THE
SKULL

· CHRISTIAN · DARKIN

A & C BLACK
AN IMPRINT OF BLOOMSBURY
LONDON   NEW DELHI   NEW YORK   SYDNEY

MEGALOSAURUS

144 MILLION YEARS AGO

She watched as a crack appeared and snaked across the perfect white surface. Finally, it was time.

She scraped away the mound of dirt uncovering one shuddering egg, then another and another. They rocked slightly in the sunlight, and she could hear her chicks calling to her from inside. Suddenly, the top of the first egg burst open. A sharp claw curled over the edge and a scaly head popped up, its eyes blinking and its tiny jaw snapping in a motion evolved to kill creatures larger than elephants. It looked at its mother, head tilted sideways, and hissed.

She leaned back, using her tail to ground her, and lifted her huge head four metres into the air. Two enormous feet dug into the earth, holding a ton of muscle in balance against the thick bone and curved, serrated teeth of her skull. Her forelimbs, small in comparison to her body, but powerful and armed with tearing claws, flexed slowly.

Beneath her, four other eggs were hatching. Her young, bristling with rough, primitive feathers, were taking their first breaths of Jurassic air, smelling the damp ferns, rotting bark, and predators and prey of the food chain that would rule their lives. A food chain which, if they were strong enough, they would climb to the very top.

The next stage of her life had begun too. Now, she was not just a hunter, she was a protector. Nothing, not even her own life, was as important as these five tiny dinosaurs. Their needs were the only thing that mattered. And their needs at the moment of hatching were clear.

They needed food.

She narrowed her eyes, sniffed the air, read the signs of the jungle, and followed the smell of living meat down to the waterhole.

Her territory was wide, but she knew its inhabitants well. She had watched the herds of bony-backed plant eaters scour the ground through the summer. She had hunted the tall duck-billed dinosaurs as they grazed among the trees. And she had followed the family of long-necked cetiosaurs that were now stooping to drink at the lake, a few metres from the dense jungle trees.

She had seen the cetiosaur mother lay her eggs, and watched the calves grow slowly for two years. The family had guarded their young closely, but despite their vigilance, one calf had been lost to a group of small nocturnal scavengers, and another had been pulled into the lake by a creature that hung just below the surface of the water. The calf that was left was the smallest, and the group slowed their pace to keep it close. She had watched and waited, but the time was never right.

Until now.

The calf was large enough to feed her and the chicks, but still small enough to take easily. And it was exposed. The adults had their heads down, drinking and could see nothing but the reflection of the sky in the water. She watched the calf wander towards her, grazing.

Oblivious.

There were many ways to make a kill. The safest was to rush headlong at the prey, mouth agape, sinking the teeth deep enough to crush bone, then pulling back, tearing open the flesh. Leaving the wound to do its work, she would follow the prey for hours or days until her victim collapsed from exhaustion, blood loss or disease.

But this was not the time for a safe hunt. Today she needed a clean kill. The young dinosaur needed to fall close enough to the nest for her to bring back chunks of meat for her chicks.

She crouched, hunger and adrenaline building within her like a coiled spring, seeping into the muscles of her legs and jaws. Her field of vision narrowed, becoming a red tunnel, every sense focused on a single point at the top of the calf's long throat. She dug her hooked claws into the ground and tensed to launch herself forward.

Before she could move, the forest around her was suddenly in motion. Flying reptiles launched themselves from every tree, fleeing with shrieks of alarm. Tiny dinosaurs scattered in every direction, feathers bristling. The cetiosaur family was on the run too. Powerful walls of flesh collided as the dinosaurs crashed into one another. The largest cetiosaur ploughed blindly through the trees, splintering them to either side. The smallest dodged and dived between its parents' legs. Every animal in the forest was united in panicked flight.

The clearing was empty in seconds. Unnerved, she swung her giant head from side to side, desperate to catch something, anything, but her jaws snapped shut on empty air. Everything was red confusion. Blood thundered in her ears. She felt the waves of heat flow over her.

It felt wrong.

She shook her head, letting her fury subside. But the world was still soaked in red light. The roaring in her ears became deafening. A fierce heat burned her back. She raised her great head and looked up into the sky.

Something was coming. A ball of fire. As if the sun was falling down.

Her instinct was to run, but she did not. This was *her* territory and her young needed her. Whatever was coming, she would stand and face it.

She felt a rush of fury, pulling every muscle taut. She planted her feet deep in the mud, braced herself against the ground, and looked directly into the fireball.

In her last second alive, she saw it. The unmistakable face of a predator. Its eyes huge, its mouth filled with piercing teeth, jaw open wide for the strike, with fire and smoke streaming from its red-hot head.

The force of the explosion turned the whole of the forest into a fine rain of ash. The thick grey flakes settled softly on the few remaining trees, left strangely upright, at the centre of the blast. They fell on her body too – lifeless, burned, but oddly undamaged, covering it where it lay until the entire valley was coated in a thick, flat layer of solidifying dust.

Above her, years passed. Centuries. Millennia. Oceans and mountains rose and fell. The dinosaurs vanished and mammals rose to fill the empty plains. She lay buried while an ape evolved and started to wonder about the mysteries of its world.

Thousands more years passed. The Roman Empire marched over her in perfectly ordered legions then, centuries later, staggered back in tatters. Behind them, they left a land of warring families, barely held together by the power of the church.

CHAPTER 1

ALFRED MARCHANT: 1176

'"And the devil is the most"...'

'"Enormous". The prior leaned over his shoulder and traced out the letters in the manuscript as he spoke.

'"Enormous of all reptiles like unto the dragon, *Draco*, which is raised in Ethiopia and India and devours elephants."' Alfred got to the end of the sentence and looked up in triumph. The prior smiled back.

'Yes,' he said. 'You will be a reader one day.'

'And a writer too,' Alfred said eagerly. 'I've been practising my name. Look.' He pulled out a scrap of dry bark on which he had scratched the words 'Alfred Marchant', in chalk.

The prior nodded slowly in approval as he held the bark up to the light of the candle.

While the prior studied the uneven scrawl, Alfred's eyes turned back to the precious book in front of him. It was not yet bound into a volume. The monks were still adding pages and would be for decades, slowly scribing out one letter at a time, illuminating each page with intricate drawings.

The book was a bestiary – a study of natural history, listing every creature the monks had seen, from the sparrow to the bear, and every animal they had heard about from travellers and legends, from the hippopotamus to the phoenix. All of known nature was to be catalogued and recorded in the monks' book. It was their great purpose.

From the moment he had first seen the fabulous creatures, the gold-lined paintings and the strange symbols, Alfred had dreamed of nothing but this book and the amazing things described in its pages. It was this obsession that drove him to learn to decipher the writing.

'I have decided to make your teaching here permanent,' the prior said, putting down Alfred's writing. 'If you would like that?'

'Yes!' whispered Alfred as he looked down at his

hands, stained red by the beetroot he'd spent the day digging. 'I would like that, very much.'

Alfred remembered his parents only vaguely. After his mother and father had died, his life had changed enormously. As a young orphan, his only value to the village was the work he could do in the fields, and that was considered little enough by the succession of families that had looked after him.

He had spent his life moving from one hut to the next and back again, as one job or another needed doing. And he knew well that in each house he moved to, he would earn only resentment from the other children who would have to share their dinner with him.

Alfred worked hard all day, and came to the monastery in the evening to study, when the other village children were playing or sleeping. He still had the long, dark walk back to the village to look forward to, but suddenly he felt elated. The prior had chosen *him* to teach. He would be a reader, maybe even a writer. Perhaps he could even live in the monastery?

The other children would be toiling for their whole lives in the same fields, but a boy who could read and write could shape his own destiny. However far his family line stretched out into the future, Alfred knew that this moment would change its direction forever.

Outside, the rain drummed against the thin leather covering the glassless window. A storm was brewing. It was the kind of night when Alfred could imagine basilisks, wolves and dragons roaming the woods.

'I'll walk you back to the village tonight,' said the prior kindly.

As they made their way through the cloisters, they found a man waiting for them at the end of a row of stone pillars. He was soaked through. The half of his face and matted hair that was visible in the yellow candlelight shone with droplets of rain. Alfred knew his name was Rolfe Nash. He looked angry, but then he was always angry. He was angry with the villagers, angry with his wife and angry with his children. He drank far more than he worked.

The prior gestured for Alfred to stay back, and stepped forward to approach Nash.

'I know what you want,' said the prior calmly, 'and the answer is still no.'

Nash mumbled something that Alfred did not hear.

'It's been a hard year for everyone's crops,' said the prior. 'But some have worked harder than others to keep them alive.'

Alfred edged closer. Nash's face was creased with anger. He was leaning in towards the prior.

'You sit up here all day while I work! What do you know about it?' Nash hissed. 'All I'm asking for is some food to put in my family's mouths! Are you going to deny me that?'

'We give help to those who need it most,' said the prior. 'But we can't give help to everyone who asks.'

Nash was holding a stone bottle. He waved it, gesturing at the walls and pillars. Outside, the old wooden structures were being slowly replaced by more solid stonework as the monastery grew. The work would have proceeded faster if there had been more than one skilled stonemason in the village.

'You're doing well for yourselves off the back of us,' Nash spat bitterly.

'We're working hard, too,' said the prior.

Nash scowled. 'And you pick and choose who to favour...' He was looking straight at Alfred, his eyes narrowed. 'While the rest of us starve!'

'We can't give to everyone who asks,' the prior said. 'And now you will have to leave.'

Nash didn't move.

'Do you want me to call the abbot away from his prayers?'

Nash hesitated, then turned his back on the prior without another word and stumbled off into the rain.

Alfred watched him go. 'It has been a bad year,' he said. 'The crops are washed out all along the valley.'

'I know,' said the prior. 'And we have more than we need here. But we don't have enough for the whole world, and so we have to choose.' He put his hand on Alfred's shoulder. 'Come on.'

They ran out from under the cover of the pillars and into the storm.

They were soaked through before they reached the woods. Above them, the wind thrashed the branches against each other, and the rain, which had fallen on to the top leaves in fine sheets, poured off again in concentrated torrents.

Underneath their feet, the ground was soft – almost liquid. As they climbed down the steep hillside on which the ancient wood grew, it seemed as if the soil was flowing away beneath them.

Alfred knew the woods well. He'd followed this route many times on his way to and from the monastery, but he never liked it. It was too dark. If you accidentally strayed off the path, thick, ancient thorn bushes tore at your hands and clothes, odd rocks sticking out of the ground tripped you, and loose overhangs hid steep and sudden drops. Although he didn't believe any of the stories the older boys told about the place, he still felt as though there was something wrong with the wood. Something menacing.

Tonight the whole place seemed alive. Even the trunks of the trees appeared to be groaning. Far off, there was a splintering crack as one old tree gave way. Alfred followed the prior closely, head down, watching his feet sink deeper into the pale mud with every step.

Deep underground, where the soil and chalk gave way to harder rock, giant sheets of limestone supported the mountain. Tonight, water was seeping through the chalk, forcing its way into cracks in the limestone, widening, fracturing and weakening the stone. On the surface, mudslides carried away smaller rocks and undermined the roots of trees. As the heavy rain continued to fall, slowly but surely, the balance of the landscape shifted.

The path wound steeply down, then equally steeply back up, and around a huge sharp rock jutting out of the hillside. Four flat stones protruded from the sodden ground, allowing the prior to quickly step up and climb around the rock. Alfred had to put both hands down into the mud to lever himself up on to each step, one at a time. As he heaved himself to a standing position on the top step, the rock began to tremble under his feet. He managed to leap off and grab hold of a bramble as the slab, nearly as large as himself, suddenly slid sideways and tumbled into the darkness.

By the time Alfred regained his footing at the top, the prior was out of sight. Alfred stared into the trees. The path was invisible, lost in a sea of darkness, mud and thrashing trees. Alfred shouted out, but he could hardly hear his own voice against the roaring of the storm. He fought the panic rising in his stomach and struggled in the rough direction of the path, hoping to catch sight of the prior's dark robes ahead, but there was nothing. It was as though the prior had been swallowed by the storm.

Suddenly the lightning rescued him. A flash and an almost instantaneous crash of thunder shook the ground. Light exploded around him. The trees in front of him were lit up, and beyond them, high up where the sloping backbone of the hill met the sky, not one, but two figures were silhouetted against the night.

One was the prior. The other, Rolfe Nash. In the brief flash of light, Alfred saw Nash's fist, clenched and shaking. His mouth wide open, teeth bared in a shout. Without thinking, Alfred grasped the ground and hauled himself onwards, towards the angry man.

As he got closer, he could see Nash shouting over the roar of the storm. He was clearly ranting. The prior said nothing – even if Nash had stopped for long enough to let him speak, it would have made no difference.

Alfred was still in the shadow of the trees. If he came forward, at least Nash would know the prior wasn't alone in the forest. He took a deep breath and was about to step out of the shadows when he saw the prior's hand, waving him back. The prior couldn't see him, but must have known he was following close behind, and did not want him to be part of this argument.

Alfred stepped back and watched.

Nash seemed to be shouting louder and louder now, but Alfred could not make out his words over the howl of the storm. Nash pointed down to the village at the bottom of the hill and then gestured violently out to the fields. He leaned forward, pushing his face towards the prior.

The prior simply shook his head. Nash's hands shot out. He shoved the prior backwards onto a wide, flat rock. The rock wobbled, started to slide, then stopped abruptly, caught by some larger structure underground. The prior staggered for a moment, recovered his balance, then froze. The rock started to move again. Not suddenly this time, but slowly, steadily, as though it were a lever that had turned a great wheel deep in the ground, taking with it the whole side of the hill. Even the trees were sliding now, the ground beneath them churning like an angry river.

Then the trees started to fall. Saplings at first, then a huge old oak, older than the village, crashing into the mud. The ground was sinking faster now, massive rocks upending and tumbling downwards. A deep cliff had opened up, just a little way in front of Alfred's feet. On the other side of the growing chasm, Nash stood staring down with panic in his eyes. Below them, the prior's rock tipped. For a second, Alfred saw his arms flail, as he stepped back trying to keep his balance. Then he fell forwards, over and over, down through the widening abyss and out of sight into the darkness.

Alfred gasped, trying to take in what he'd just seen. He looked back up at Nash, and at that moment a bolt of lightning illuminated both of them. Nash was looking straight at him. Instinctively, Alfred ducked back, but it was too late. He had been seen.

Nash had just been responsible for the death of one of the most respected men in the community, and Alfred was the only one who knew it. If Alfred made it back to the village, Nash would be on trial for his life.

Alfred turned and dived back into the woods. He had a few moments' head start before Nash could find a way around the landslide, but there was still only one way down to the village, and that was through the densest part of the forest.

Branches scratched Alfred's face and legs as he ran blindly into the darkness. Away from the path, the thorny brambles grew in thick patches. He dodged one clump and leapt over another. As he swerved to avoid running into the enormous trunk of an ancient oak tree, he crashed sideways into a wide thicket of ivy and blackberry. The brambles tore at his clothes, catching around his ankles and dragging him backwards. He scrambled over the matted branches where he could, but soon found himself on the ground, on all fours, pushing underneath the thorns, ignoring the mud and the stinging nettles.

The bottom of the thicket was easier to fight through than the top. The plants grew towards the light, and the underside of the brambles were dark and thin. Even so, Nash would be close behind, and Alfred was sure he was making so much noise that he would be easily heard even against the storm.

He scrambled on through the mud. Suddenly the brambles opened out into a tunnel just wide enough for him to crawl through, and Alfred dived into it. It was almost made for him, winding through the thorn bushes, forking and dividing as he pushed his way onwards. He knew immediately what these tunnels were; he had read about them in the prior's bestiary. They were the trails made by badgers searching for food. He knew that they would lead from the badger's sett out to the edge of the thicket. As long as he was moving in the right direction, he would eventually find a way out.

Abruptly, the thorns gave way, and Alfred was back in open woodland. He clambered to his feet and started to run. He had no idea where he was, but the village was at the bottom of the hill, so he headed downwards. The hillside was steep, and he had to zigzag back and forth to avoid falling headlong. His lungs were gasping and his heart beating fast. Around him, the storm was still at its height. The wind blew leaves and sticks and rain in gusts from every direction, and the loose mud and stones threatened to topple him at every turn.

He struggled to hear sounds of pursuit over the gale, but every sound could have been Nash's shouting. His eyes tried to focus on the jumping shadows as he fought his way down the hill, but each time he thought he saw a hand reaching out at him or a cloak billowing, it turned out to be just a branch waving violently or a frightened animal scurrying off into the night.

Under his feet, the ground suddenly levelled out. He had hit the path. He pelted along the wet, slippery surface as fast as he could, at last able to run without worrying that he would hit a tree. The path turned downwards in a familiar arc. In an instant he knew where he was. Just a few more turns, back and forth along the hillside, then a sharp straight drop and the road would level out into the village.

Alfred took a great gulp of air. It felt as though he'd been holding his breath without even realising it. He followed the path, picking up speed. The path made a sharp bend around four solid tree trunks, blocking his view, but he knew it well.

He leaned in around the bend and smashed straight into Nash's open arms. Alfred crashed into him so hard and so fast that they both went flying to the ground. Nash tried to grab him. Alfred flailed and struggled. He jumped to his feet, but Nash gripped his ankle and he twisted and fell again. Nash was on his feet now, and stooping over to get hold of him. Alfred kicked his legs hard against the man's chest, and the force of it pushed the boy off the path and onto the muddy slope. Suddenly he was rolling over and over. Mud and stones were sliding around him, as he half-skidded, half-fell down the hill. Behind him, Nash was shouting and cursing, but he couldn't follow. His furious yells disappeared into the storm.

Abruptly, Alfred's fall stopped. The trees and the hillside were at an end, and he lay in the grass, exhausted.

Now he felt the rain again. It was coming down almost in solid sheets, but he didn't care. He could see the first huts of the village, hear the animals inside, almost feel their warmth. For as long as he could remember, he had never thought of the village as somewhere he belonged. It was somewhere to escape from. But tonight, it felt like home.

Above him a single star shone through a tiny break in the cloud. The prior had pointed it out to him one night. Mars. He fixed his eyes on it, forced them to focus, as if that effort alone could draw him up out of the mud.

With one last effort, he pulled himself to his feet, still staring upwards. His ankles and his knees were weak and bruised, and he could feel the scratches on his face and legs as he stumbled towards the nearest hut.

As he pushed his way in, he was barely aware of the people huddled inside. He swayed on his feet, and saw someone step forward to catch him as he fell.

'The prior...' he managed as the darkness swam around him. 'Nash has killed the prior!'

CHAPTER 2

ALFRED MARCHANT: 1176

By the time Alfred awoke, the storm was over, and the dawn was clear and bright. The whole village was gathered outside the hut as he emerged to tell his story. He knew everyone. He had grown up with them, but he had always felt like an outsider.

It seemed to Alfred that the village was irrevocably tied to the sequence of planting the fields: beetroot, then beans, then fallow, then back to beetroot again. Over and over, year after year, going back as far as anyone could remember, and on and on forever. Nothing else seemed to concern them; it was all they knew and all they wanted to know. The fact that Alfred was, by some accident, better than most at growing beetroot and beans meant he was fed and kept, but these crops were something he wanted to leave behind. He wanted a different kind of future, and last night, with the prior's kind offer, it had almost become a reality.

But that was all over now, of course. All the future would hold for him would be beetroot and beans… forever. All the youngest faces he saw around him had already sworn themselves to be his enemies. He had worked for most of their parents in return for a share of food and shelter, and the children had learned to hate him for it.

The parents' faces were not set as hard against him, but he knew they were suspicious of the time he spent at the monastery. The monks were rich enough to give charity to those they chose, and powerful enough to make rules for the villagers, but the books they read and wrote were viewed as a dangerous mystery by most of the farmers. Alfred had tried to explain what the bestiary was, but his talk of dragons and creatures that could turn you to stone just by looking at you only seemed to make things worse.

He started to tell the crowd about how the prior had offered to walk with him through the storm, and how Nash had waited for them on the hillside. As he spoke, he realised something strange was happening.

The adults' expressions begin to change. They might be suspicious of Alfred and of the prior, but they all knew Nash, and they had all seen his anger.

When Alfred described how Nash had pushed the prior and the landslide had taken him, he was sure he could see understanding, even sympathy, in their eyes. For the first time in years, he began to feel he was a part of the village. His voice became stronger. He started to almost enjoy his story as he recounted how he'd fled through the thickets, fought off Nash, and then rolled down the hill and into the village.

By the time he had finished, even the other children were staring, open-mouthed, willing him on. Alfred was smiling now. He couldn't believe it. They were actually listening to him. Taking notice of him. He wasn't just a necessary nuisance, another one of the animals to be fed and worked. He was one of them.

The stonemason brought him back to earth.

'Well…' he said slowly, 'I suppose we've got a body to find.' He brushed his huge hands down a burned and oily leather apron. 'And a murderer.'

If the prior had been organising the search, everyone would have spread out in a long line along the bottom of the hill, and worked their way up, searching every bush until they reached the monastery at the top. Every inch of the forest would have been covered and nothing, or no one, would have escaped the search.

As it was, most of the younger farmers strode out into the woods hefting spades and heavy sticks. Behind them, the older men started up the main path, while the rest of the villagers picked their way up the side of the hill in loose groups, shouting out randomly as they lost sight of each other.

The wood was filled with their calling, and for a moment Alfred felt strangely proud that all this action was taking place because of him. Until he remembered that the prior was dead and that Nash, unless he had fled, was still somewhere on the hillside.

Alfred led the stonemason and young farmers up the hillside, following the route down which he had slid and rolled the previous night. Finally they reached the path where he and Nash had fought.

The mud showed signs of a struggle. Alfred saw something stuck fast in a muddy puddle. He pulled it out. It was Nash's shoe. The leather was nearly worn through, and the sodden moss used to pad the inside fell out in great clumps as he lifted it.

'He won't have got far without that,' said the stonemason. He looked down the path towards the four heavy trees around which Alfred had run the previous night. Their thick leaves would have offered shelter against the rain. 'This way,' he said.

He led the group up the grass bank and around behind the trees, and then shouted.

Propped up against the tree trunk and unconscious, a body lay slumped in drunken slumber. It was Nash.

As the group gathered round, the stonemason pulled the drunk roughly to his feet, and Nash started to wake. He grunted as he looked at the faces crowding around him, then panicked and fought weakly for a few seconds. But the stonemason's hands were used to far tougher work. Suddenly, Nash shook his head and focused on Alfred.

'Murderer!' he screeched, wrenching an arm free and stabbing it at Alfred. 'Witch! Witch!'

Alfred flinched in horror. If an accusation of witchcraft was taken seriously, it would mean a witch trial – even torture and execution. The villagers already mistrusted the prior and his books. While nobody dared challenge the monks' authority, Alfred was just a boy, and an unpopular one at that. If anyone had a grudge to settle, here was their chance.

There was a long silence. A crowd was gathering around the tree. Alfred held his breath. At last, the stonemason spoke. 'And I suppose you're an angel an' all?' he boomed. The crowd laughed, and Alfred let out a huge sigh.

There was no doubt in his mind now. Something had changed for him today.

Alfred pushed on up the hill. The stonemason kept pace with him, while the others followed, dragging the cursing Nash with them. The only thing left to do was to find the prior. The mudslide had taken him down the far side of the hill, and as they neared the top, they could see the gap left by the trees that had been carried away when the ground subsided.

The group crossed the crest of the hill in silence before they reached the top, and headed down and around to the bottom of the landslide area. Alfred dreaded what he would find there. The prior had been the nearest thing Alfred had to family. Only a few hours ago, he had promised to take Alfred into his care, to teach him. Had the prior told any of the other monks about his decision? Would they honour it? Alfred had no idea.

Suddenly, up ahead, Alfred could see gaps in the trees that had not been there yesterday. Villagers were standing between the trees, staring in silence down into a new clearing. At first, Alfred couldn't see what they were looking at. A crowd blocked his way, and he was too short to see over them. He ran forward, pushed his way through, and stumbled out into the sunlight.

The landslide had carved a strip of mud like a freshly ploughed field all the way from the top of the hill to the bottom. Every tree that had stood in its path had been uprooted, and was now piled in broken splinters at the bottom of the hill. The villagers had gathered at either side of the clearing in two long rows, none of them daring to step forward into the mudslide's path.

Alfred stood alone, ankle deep in the mud. Looking back, he could see only the crowd's horrified faces. The stonemason stood among them, his great hands covering his mouth in shock. As Alfred watched, he turned and and started to run, pounding his way up the hill. Terrified, Alfred turned slowly to face the centre of the clearing. There was the prior's body. Mud and blood soaking his clothes, he was lying bent over backwards, held up clear of the ground by a huge lump of rock.

But it was not a rock.

At the bottom of the mass of stone, the shape of a vast empty eye-socket was visible above the mud. Higher up, the stone tapered to form a blunt snout, lined with curved, serrated teeth. The massive mouth was frozen, gaping open, and the whole skull was embedded in grey rock as though the earth had grown around it like flesh and muscle. The terrifying jaws formed a deep crevice in the boulder on which the prior had landed, his fragile body impaled on its terrible sharp teeth.

It seemed as though a dragon had reared out of the ground in the night, grabbed the prior in its teeth, and then been turned to stone by the first rays of the dawn sun.

She had claimed her first victim in a hundred million years.

Scattered around the bloodied stone were the contents of the bag the prior always carried with him. Rough scraps covered in unreadable symbols and sketched drawings of strange creatures. Alfred recognised them as practice scribbles for the great book, but the villagers saw only mysterious and dangerous incantations.

Suddenly, Nash's harsh voice burst out. 'Witch!' he cried. 'Witch!' His captors had released their grip on him and he lurched into the clearing. 'Witch!' he shouted again.

Slowly, the villagers' eyes started to turn away from the prior's body and towards Alfred. Whispers started to hiss through the air. Alfred heard the word again from somewhere else in the crowd. 'Witch! Witch!'

Then again, louder this time, from the other side of the clearing. 'Witch! Sorcerer!'

The faces before Alfred were hardening like the terrible stone creature behind him. 'Witch! Witch!' The chorus grew, getting louder and louder. Children were shouting, the men pounding their sticks against the trees.

Alfred tried to protest, but he could barely hear his own voice above the repeated shouts. Two of the men who had been restraining Nash stepped forward and grabbed him by the shoulders. In a panic, he tried to struggle, but their fingers dug deep into his flesh, pinning him to the spot. He looked wildly around. Even if he managed to break free, he was surrounded by the whole village. Everyone here wanted him dead. He didn't stand a chance.

Nash stepped out in front of him. He was holding a rusty knife, and it was raised above his head. He was about to bring it down.

Suddenly, Nash froze, and looked up the hillside. The crowd's chanting died away, and behind it, a quieter, more melodic chant rose up.

Alfred looked up. Along the top of the hill, dark, shapes were emerging. The monks. He could just make out the stonemason pointing down towards the prior's body as he led them towards Alfred and the villagers.

The abbot stopped the procession in the middle of the clearing. He raised his hands high and waited for the crowd to fall silent. 'We will take the boy with us,' he announced.

Alfred had been digging for weeks under the instruction of the new prior and the stonemason, but there was so much still to do. He had flattened out the ground around the dragon's skull, so that the side of the hill now had a huge, solid step carved into it.

Over the following years, Alfred would dig foundations as the stonemason taught him his craft. He would learn how to hew stone into blocks, and around the skull, he would build a tomb.

The monks understood it as his education – learning a craft. The villagers understood it as a penance. A punishment for his crime, although what his exact crime was, no one would say.

For Alfred, building the tomb was part of the deal that the monks had struck with the villagers to allow him to live. He had gone to stay with them in the monastery that fateful day, and as the prior had promised, he was also learning to read and write.

Day after day, week after week, Alfred returned to the skull's resting place. As he stared into the huge empty eye socket of the creature, it was almost as if the monster was looking right back at him, asking him questions he could never answer in his lifetime. As he worked in its gaze, he felt as though it was somehow shaping him. Filling him with a desire for knowledge that he would pass on to his children, and his children's children...

The tomb stood solid while centuries passed. The village was destroyed, rebuilt, and destroyed and rebuilt again. Softened by wind, rain and moss, Alfred's stonework remained unchanged as the woods grew back around it, while the fierce creature buried in its depths lay forgotten.

Waiting.

CHAPTER 3

THOMAS MARCHANT: 1535

That was the problem, Thomas Marchant thought, as he watched his father argue with a stallholder. When you came to buy provisions for the monastery, everyone always assumed you had plenty of money. The stallholder could see their horse was a good one, and he could see the empty cart it pulled. It didn't take much to work out they'd come to town to stock up for the monks. That, in most people's eyes, meant you could afford to pay twice what everyone else paid for the same food.

Unfortunately, things had changed. Henry VIII was no friend of the monks, nor of the libraries they protected. He had been slowly choking them for years; now things were getting worse by the week.

The few monks who tried to keep the monasteries and libraries going were forced to lead the king's men in a desperate dance, trying to hide anything of value from the constant inspections, surveys and taxes. Thomas knew his father could earn twice what the monks paid him as a stonemason anywhere else, but for some reason he seemed determined to stay, working constantly to stop the crumbling monastery from finally falling down. Nobody ever said out loud that the king's death was the only thing that could save them, but there was constant talk about his wounded leg, his open sores, and the fact that he needed servants to carry him from his bed to his chair.

Thomas' father held out his purse. 'Look,' he said, in desperation. 'This is all I have. There is no more. This should buy me everything you have here.'

The stallholder didn't flinch. 'You can have half of what's here,' he said. 'That's my price. You can always go somewhere else.'

'Somewhere else' was at least three hours' ride away, and it was already starting to get dark. They would have to buy from him or go home with nothing, and the stallholder knew it.

Just then, Thomas noticed something odd out of the corner of his eye. On the other side of the square, another cart had arrived. Its contents had hay strewn over them, and the driver looked anxious and jumpy, but he had stopped next to the other market stalls, so he clearly had something to sell. A small crowd was gathering, rummaging in the cart.

The man in the cart looked around nervously, then held something up for everyone to see. It was a book. Not a printed book – an old book. Leather bound. Inlaid with intricate designs. The sort of book that only nobles or monasteries owned. But the man was clearly neither a noble nor a monk.

Thomas' father had given up arguing. He had opened the purse and was just about to tip the contents into the stallholder's waiting hands when Thomas grabbed his father's arm and pointed across the square.

Instantly, his father closed the purse and started to run towards the bookseller with Thomas close behind.

By the time Thomas reached the cart, his father had pushed the covering of hay aside. Underneath, dozens of books lay in piles. Some were modern block-print books, but others were church books – handwritten and painstakingly bound. They did not belong here.

'Where did these come from?' Thomas' father demanded. The answer was obvious. There was only one place they could have come from – a monastery.

The bookseller looked harried. 'A place up north,' he said vaguely. 'The king's men had already been and gone with anything worth having. There was nobody there. Just gangs of looters wrecking the place.'

'And you,' said Thomas' father, dryly.

'I could either take the books or leave them to burn,' snapped the man.

Thomas looked at his father. 'We're here to buy food,' he reminded him.

'I know,' said his father slowly, fingering the purse in his hands. 'But...' He turned to the man. 'I'll give you everything here for the lot.' He opened the purse.

The man blinked at the money. Thomas could tell he wanted to get rid of his wares as quickly as possible, but he was hesitating. The bookseller was no fool, and knew what the old books were worth. Thomas looked at the mangy old drayhorse that dragged the man's rickety cart, then back at their strong workhorse. He'd known her as long as he could remember. He swallowed hard. 'And we'll take your horse and cart for ours,' he heard himself say.

The man grabbed the purse and took off across the square. Thomas' father stared at him. He shrugged.

'Come on.' His father smiled grimly. 'We've got to warn the monks. It's starting.'

Thomas shuffled on the hard wooden planks of the cart as it bumped and rocked slowly along the rough track. He'd shoved a pile of straw underneath him, but it wasn't making much difference. The sun had gone down and Mars was bright in the sky, arcing slowly over their heads in the opposite direction to the rest of the stars. It didn't light their way, but they followed it towards home. His father kept urging the old horse on, but didn't say much as they started to climb the hill into the wood.

'Is that going to happen to our monastery?' Thomas asked.

'I think so, now. Yes.' Thomas could tell it was hard for his father to even say it.

'What will we do?'

'I'll find work easily enough. The important thing is, we need to save the library. These books have to be for everyone, otherwise nothing will change. One day, everyone will be able to read, and everyone will have the power, and then kings and queens will have to obey their subjects.'

Thomas looked back at the books strewn amongst the hay in the back of the cart. The library they came from was in ruins now, and the same thing was happening all over England. He thought of the monastery where he and his father lived, and how the villagers came there to learn to read. The common people were being educated, and the nobles were getting scared.

The cart lurched up the long winding path on to the brow of the hill. The old horse was struggling, but as it reached the top, the path levelled out and the going got easier. Suddenly, the trees thinned out and they could see sky ahead. The moon illuminated the hillside, outlining the clouds in silver. Ahead, a dark plume of thick smoke rose up in to the sky, lit from below by a flickering orange glow.

The monastery was burning.

Instantly, Thomas' father leapt out of the cart and started running up the hill towards the smoke. 'Go now!' he shouted back to Thomas. 'Hide. I'll find you in the morning.' And with that he was gone.

His father had to do what he could, but of course, the monastery would be lost now. There could be soldiers, looters, anyone up there. The place was being burned to the ground for nothing more valuable than the lead on its roof. Thomas knew he should keep out of the way until it was all over. And yet... In the back of the cart, gold thread traced a pattern woven into one of the books' bindings. It shone in the moonlight.

At least he could save these books if he could find a safe place to hide them.

And he knew of one place that was very safe indeed.

Thomas peered down into the wood. It was nearly pitch black, but through the trees, he could just make out the outline of the old tomb in the moonlight. The other villagers were scared of the place and told dark stories about it. They said it was a prison for a demon, or some such nonsense, but to Thomas it held no terror. To him, it was where he practised his skills with stone. While his father repaired the monastery walls, he was given the job of keeping the tomb secure. On its walls he had learned to shore up, to replace and to carve – just as his father had, and his father before him. The old tomb was a patchwork of the labour of generations of stonemasons, each adding their own new ideas and fixing ancient mistakes. It was less of a building, and more of a conversation with his ancestors: a window back through time to whoever laid the first stones.

Through his work on the tomb, Thomas knew one thing that nobody else in the world knew. He knew some of the stones around the doorway were loose. Now was the time to finally open it.

There was no path to the tomb, and although Thomas had hauled enough stone blocks down the slope to know there was enough space for a cart to pass through, he'd never made the trip in the dark. The old horse struggled and stumbled as he climbed out of the cart and started to lead it over the brow of the hill and down towards the stone monument.

He picked his way carefully, feeling for the flattest route as the cart behind him lurched dangerously from side to side. The slope was perilous and steep, and he had to manoeuvre the frightened animal carefully around each rock and tree. If the cart tipped over now, it would drag them both tumbling down the hill to their deaths.

Eventually, they made it. The ground levelled out, and Thomas quickly found the doorway of the tomb and felt around for the loose stones at the top. They seemed firm at first touch, but that was only because he'd wedged them into place to prevent the damage getting worse before he could make a proper repair.

Thomas edged out the shards of rock he'd pressed into the gaps, then slowly rocked a loose stone until the mud and brittle mortar around it fell away.

Climbing on top of the tomb, he braced himself against the stone roof, and pushed the loose stone with his heels. It rocked, but held. He pushed again and slowly the stone shifted out of position, toppling to the ground with a loud thump.

He peered inside nervously. It was a void as dark as the space between stars. With one stone removed, the others around it fell more easily, and soon there was a space wide enough for him to squeeze through. Filling his father's leather bag with as many of the books as he could, Thomas felt his way into the damp blackness. He almost tripped on what seemed to be rough steps leading down to an inner chamber. No matter how much his eyes strained, he could see nothing but the jagged rectangle of starlight through which he'd climbed.

Tentatively, he felt his way along one wall. It felt oddly rough. The smooth, hewn stone seemed to have been cut and joined to a huge crag of broken rock – as though the tomb had been built around something else. Why would a mason do that?

Further along the wall, the rough rock was ridged with smooth, curved shapes. His expert hands traced them. Jutting curved triangles arranged in a row diagonally down the wall. They couldn't have been carved, he knew that from their texture, but they were like nothing he'd ever felt in a natural rock.

Suddenly, Thomas felt cold. He had never believed what the villagers said about the tomb, but there was definitely something hidden here. Something he did not understand. He had to get out. He tipped the books onto the floor, scrambled up the steps, and climbed out through the hole into the bright darkness of the wood.

It was nothing, he told himself, breathing heavily for a few moments while his heartbeat slowed down. Just stone. In any case, there were more books. He would have to go back. He loaded the remaining books into the shoulder bag. This time, he took a lamp and tinderbox he had found stowed in the back of the cart, before climbing through the hole and into the void.

Gingerly, Thomas made his way down the steps, and placed the books quietly on the floor. He opened the tinderbox, and struck the flint against the steel, sending a cluster of impossibly bright sparks flying into the air. He struck it again and a spark landed on the char-cloth in his hand, making it glow. He screwed the cloth up and blew on it, then touched the end to the lamp, and a flame grew slowly into life.

As his eyes adjusted to the flickering flame, the

tomb began to reveal itself to him. There was no casket. No bones. No artefacts. The floor was of flat stones. The roof held no carvings. The walls were not decorated.

And yet, Thomas suddenly saw the tomb was not empty. He gasped and staggered back.

One entire wall was built around a huge cracked boulder, and across its surface, ridges of stone traced the shape of a huge, open jaw, lined with curved teeth reaching up toward the sky. Below them a round, empty eye-socket glared out, shifting in the flickering lamp-light so that it appeared to hold a dark pupil, darting and flicking like the eye of a crow.

Thomas controlled his breathing and as the shock subsided, he felt something else. Not fear, but curiosity. This was the demon that the villagers whispered about, sure enough. But it was stone, and Thomas knew stone. His mind was filled not with fear that the creature would rise suddenly into life, but with wonder at how stone could be worked into these shapes.

It was an incredible, beautiful thing, but he had no idea how it could have been created.

Slowly, he sat, and for a long time just stared at it. The huge eye gazed sightlessly back at him. The books lay scattered on the floor around him. Time seemed to pass both quickly and not at all, as if there was nothing else in the world.

Here was something he simply knew nothing about, yet it had been here all along, so close to him for his entire life, and his father's life, and his father's before that. Silent. Waiting. He had read all about the history of the monastery in the library, but not one book had mentioned the old tomb. Yet someone had built it. Thomas had felt his hand as he had worked on the stones – he had felt as though he knew him. But that first tomb builder had known about the face in the rock, and his knowledge had somehow been lost, buried all these years. How could that happen?

The answer was simple enough. Thomas knew nothing of it because nobody had written it down.

Staring into the great eye, a realisation stirred and rose inside him. Everything he had learned in his life would be lost the same way if the monastery library burned tonight.

Thomas grabbed the lamp and hauled himself out of the tomb. He knew exactly what he had to do.

By the time he had coaxed and shouldered the old horse and its cart up towards the edge of the woods where the trees came closest to the monastery wall, the night was at its darkest. Driving a horse and cart through the wood without using the road would have been difficult even in daylight, and doing it in darkness was almost impossible. The night was still and every sound made him freeze and stare into the shadows, searching for the shape of a figure or the glint of a sword.

When he saw the glow of the fire through the trees and felt the heat in the air, he left the horse and cart where he hoped they wouldn't be seen, and crept to the edge of the trees.

The monastery was fully ablaze, the windows pouring smoke and flames into the night sky. The lead roof of the hall was melting. A hole had opened up and the tiles at the edges were bending downwards, sliding, dripping into the flames. The wooden supports holding up the roof up were burning too, and as Thomas watched, one great beam gave way in a splintering shower of sparks. As it fell, the rest of the roof started to tilt downwards, and one after another, the remaining beams snapped, the whole roof caving slowly into the fire.

On the ground was chaos. People were running back and forth, frantically loading carts and bags with whatever they could carry. One man had his arms full of crockery from the kitchens. Another man had a wall hanging draped over his shoulder.

Thomas couldn't tell who were monks, who were looters and who were the king's men. Everyone was simply getting away with what they could. Down at the front of the building, he recognised the prior and his father, arguing with a tall man who looked as though he was directing some of the other men. Whatever they were saying, it was having little effect on the looters who were sifting through a pile of furniture and oddments.

Thomas shifted his gaze over to the library at the back of the building. Luckily, it seemed to have been pretty much ignored by the looters, but there was a wisp of smoke drifting out of the top of the left-hand window.

He kept low to the ground as he darted out of the wood and across what had been the vegetable garden, flattening himself against the building. He could feel the heat of the fire through the stone walls as he edged along and round into the darkness at the back of the library.

The thin windows would have been too narrow for an adult to squeeze through, which was probably why the looters had abandoned the library after smashing the windows and ripping out the lead linings. However, Thomas was smaller. With a grunt, he managed to pull himself up on to the narrow frame and drop down on to the floor inside.

The only door to the rest of the building was securely locked, but smoke was pouring in underneath it and filling the room. It looked as though it could burst open at any moment, flooding the room with fire and choking fumes.

The books were still there. The newer, less precious volumes were kept in a bookcase near the window. They were arranged in rows with their spines facing the wall so that they could be taken out and opened without tangling the metal chains that locked them to the shelves. The more valuable handwritten books were chained to rows of solid oak desks. Thomas grabbed a book and yanked at it, but it held firm. He wasn't going to be able to break the chains or move the desks, so he turned his attention to the bookcase. He grabbed at the side and pulled. It moved a little. Puffing and panting, he prised it from the wall, and dragged one end and then the other, until the bookcase stood side-on in front of the window. It looked like it might just fit through, if he could lift it.

He grabbed the bottom, and heaved with all his might. It tilted a little then slammed back down on his fingers. He put his shoulder against it and tried again. This time he got it a little higher before it crashed back down. One more try... Thomas put his fingers underneath the bottom shelf, his feet against a desk, and heaved. The bookcase lifted. His feet slid and scrabbled against the floor as he leaned into the wooden cabinet and heaved again.

Slowly, the bookcase tilted upward, then over, the far side crashing down on the window sill with the edge sticking out into the night. Thomas lifted the bottom and pushed hard until the case slid out, pivoted on the window sill, and smashed upside down on to the ground outside.

The smoke was getting thicker now, and tongues of orange flame had begun to flicker under the door. Thomas looked around for something that might break the chains holding the books to the desks. He remembered that his father had been working on a tile in the corner of the room just before they'd left for the market. If he was lucky, he might have left some of his tools behind...

He had.

Thomas recognised a cloth bag left neatly in the

corner beside a cracked stone. Inside were a small chisel and a hammer. He scooped them up and aimed a blow at the chain nearest him, pinning it against the floor. The floor tile cracked, but the chain held. He hit it again and it folded in two. Another blow, and the link split. He grabbed the book, threw it out of the window and moved on to the next one.

He was keeping low to avoid the smoke and trying to hold his breath for as long as he could, but his eyes were stinging and he was starting to feel dizzy. He freed two more books and took a gulp of air at the window as he threw them outside, but as he turned to go back for more, the room suddenly exploded in a ball of fire. Half of the door flew across the room and splintered on the wall next to his head. The other half crashed on to a desk and an ancient, handwritten bible bound in leather and gold erupted into flames.

Thomas knew he had to get out. The heat was unbearable and the smoke was closing in around him. But out of the corner of his eye, he saw it. The bestiary, lying open on a desk on the far side of the room. It was the treasure of the monastery. The work of years – generations, even. A dragon's tail curled across the open page, and a huge eye glared out at him from behind rows of curved teeth.

He took a deep breath at the window and forced himself back into the room. His face stung with the heat, and he could barely see as he stumbled towards the flames. Reaching out, he grabbed the chain holding the book. It was almost too hot to touch, and as he raised his hammer and struck at it, he could see the fire spreading up the leg of the desk.

His first blow missed entirely, while his second only dented the metal chain. He could feel himself getting weaker with each passing second. The flames and the heat were relentless. His head swam as he aimed another strike, and another.

As he swung the hammer down for a final attempt, the chain snapped, and at the same moment, the dragon on the page burst into flames. Desperately, Thomas heaved at the chain, flinging the burning book towards the window. It arced through the air and out into the garden, still burning.

Thomas' lungs were bursting as he hauled himself to the window, on to the sill and out into the darkness. He landed hard on his hands and knees and gulped mouthfuls of air, coughing and choking and rubbing the smoke out of his eyes.

Slowly, he shook the dizziness from his head and scrambled to his feet. Beside him, the bestiary was lying in the mud, burned almost to nothing. Its binding was charred. Its pages, thousands of hours of work, were nothing more than blackened scraps of ash. Thomas picked it up, but the binding disintegrated in his hands. There was nothing left to save. Instead, he turned to the other volumes piled beside the window – at least they were safe for now. He grabbed the three loose volumes, and ran with them back to the woods, throwing them into the cart.

The crowd of looters was beginning to thin out now, and the sky was starting to brighten. The king's hired thugs had managed to scare most of them off, and were wandering about in small groups, looking for anything left worth taking. Thomas knew he had to get going. He didn't have time to break the chains of all the books, and he would never be able to get the cabinet across to the woods unnoticed.

There was only one thing to be done. Creeping back to where the bookcase was lying in the grass, he wrapped his shirt around the chisel to deaden the sound and tapped as quietly as he could at the corners of the shelves, dislodging them from the cabinet one by one. Once they were all free, he grabbed the shelves two at a time and ran, dragging the books behind him across the garden and into the woods. Twice he saw groups of the king's men rounding the corner of the burning building, and twice he dropped to the ground, lying unnoticed until they had passed. Eventually, he made it to the woods with all the books and loaded them into the cart.

The journey back to the tomb was quicker and easier. The horse was beginning to learn its way and trust him, and the sun was starting to rise. By the time it was fully light, Thomas had safely stowed all the books in the tomb.

He must have climbed into the back of the cart and fallen asleep in the hay, because the next thing he felt was his father's hand on his shoulder.

He sat up and rubbed his eyes, still stinging from the smoke. His father's face was black, his clothes filthy and torn. He had a defeated look in his eyes.

'It's lost,' he said, his voice cracking. 'All of it gone, burned or stolen. Even the library... There's nothing left, son.'

'Yes there is,' cried Thomas. He grabbed his father's arm, led him to the tomb and pointed through the hole where the sunlight shone down, illuminating the books piled on the floor.

His father stared in disbelief.

'I couldn't save everything,' said Thomas. 'But I tried. I really did try.'

Later, as they headed down towards the village, tired and hungry, Thomas' father drove the cart in silence. Thomas could see he was turning things over and over in his head. Finally, he spoke. 'Our lives are going to be dangerous now. We can never tell anyone where the books are, but we have to use them... they have to be seen. To be read. To teach people. Otherwise they may as well have burned.'

The previous night had been the end of everything Thomas had ever known, but somehow this morning felt like a beginning. Yesterday the library was crumbling and doomed. Today there was a new library. A secret library in a tomb guarded by a monster. And Thomas Marchant and his family were its keepers.

CHAPTER 4

WILLIAM MARCHANT 1693

William Marchant looked around the table at the faces flickering in the candlelight. Were they serious? Did they really still believe this stuff?

They weren't stupid. More than half of them could read, thanks to his secret library. And yet the head of every farming family in the village was sitting around the table, leaning in to hear what the old white witch had to say.

Juliana let her audience wait in silence for a long time before opening her bag and pulling out a finger-sized wooden statue of a veiled goddess and placing it deliberately in the centre of the table. It made a loud hollow sound.

William opened his mouth, but quickly shut it

again as he caught a sideways look from his mother Elizabeth, sitting at the head of the table. She was reminding him that he had to be careful. He only had a place at the meeting because it was taking place at his home, and what he had to say was far too important to say badly.

He looked around at the faces, and his feelings softened a little. Juliana did know a fair bit, it was true, and she was harmless enough. She had earned respect in the village, despite her son's job. It was to her that everyone in the village went when they were sick, desperate, or when they feared for the future. Somehow she usually helped them to feel better.

Right now, the whole village was desperate and fearful. If the early seeds they had planted didn't grow fast and strong, there would be death from starvation in every house.

Perhaps it was not belief that made them listen to her, but lack of anything else in which to put their faith.

The little statue stood in the centre of the table while Juliana explained how the crops would return if only the Great Mother, the Goddess Freya or the Virgin Mary – she seemed to use the names interchangeably – blessed and looked over the crops.

Everyone stared in silence at the tiny figure, while Juliana described in detail how villages in northern France ensured their harvests by a ritual in which they took their goddess statue on a tour of the fields as they sowed them. They danced and sang for the wooden idol, and gave tribute. And in return, the goddess, by whatever name you called her, blessed the fields and the crops grew strong and tall.

In William's opinion, such superstition was ridiculous, but at the mention of northern France the assembled farmers looked at each other, nodding sagely. Everyone knew that the crops over the Channel were thriving, and everyone wondered why those few short miles of sea made such a difference.

Everyone also knew, although they were far too careful to mention it, that one among them was something of an expert on northern France. And everyone was looking at William now. He cleared his throat. The library and the monster were not his only secrets. It was well known, though rarely discussed, that Elizabeth was able to acquire foreign trinkets for the villagers, and that she would often pay over the odds for sacks of wool, which then strangely disappeared. The villagers assumed that her son somehow managed to evade the coastguard, and make a small living selling smuggled wool to the French, but it was in nobody's best interest to know for certain where he went when he disappeared for days on end. And absolutely nobody knew what or whom he brought back when he returned.

He swallowed and started to speak. 'The French crops don't grow because of magic and spells,' he said as levelly as he could. 'They grow because of this.' He pulled out a small bag, and upended it on the middle of the table. A cascade of beans rattled out, surrounding the little statue and rolling into the curious hands of the villagers.

They were much darker and richer-looking than the seeds the farmers were used to planting, and William watched their brows wrinkle as they assessed them.

'I was... um... given them by someone who visited France,' he continued, allowing himself a small smile at what everyone knew was a lie. 'They're stronger than the seeds we use here, and they harvest earlier. They also improve the soil for next year's crops.'

He looked around the room, but nobody spoke. He could tell that he'd lost them. When harvests failed, it seemed most farmers could easily believe their crops had been sabotaged by evil spirits. Trying to persuade them to accept that, in fact, they were planting the wrong kind of seeds seemed wholly impossible.

There was a long silence, and one by one the farmers shifted their gaze back from the seeds to the little statue. William looked at his mother, and she shrugged helplessly.

'We should put our trust in the power of the Lady,' said Juliana. The others started to nod.

'This? This is going to bless our crops?' The words burst out of William. He picked up the statue in his fingers. 'This is going to save our village? This little charm is going to feed us?' He tossed it back onto the table, exasperated.

Juliana smiled. 'It won't, of course. The boy's right.' She was in control now and she knew it. 'With this we can bless but a few grains of seed. That's all.'

'Then what exactly are you asking of us?' Elizabeth's tone was open and friendly, but her question was impossible to dodge.

'We need a much older, more powerful Lady,' Juliana said. 'In France they have a cart. They have used it for centuries. Inside is the image of the Lady and her tributes. They add a sheaf from the last harvest, flowers, some other magic tokens.' William rolled his eyes. 'They take her from village to village to bless the crops.' She looked around the room. 'When have the French crops failed? Never!'

Juliana was looking only at William now. Her voice was softer. 'If only there was someone who could trade with the French, purchase a loan of the cart and fetch it back here – just for a week, to bestow her blessings on our fields.'

Surely she was joking. William knew the farmers in France well enough, and there were at least a couple who might sneak the cart out for him and down to the shore if he could promise to get it back in a week or two, but it would take a hefty bribe. It would bankrupt the village – and for what?

William stood up. He had no more than opened his mouth to make it clear what he thought of the old woman's plan when the door banged open on its hinges and a young man in a green coat appeared in the doorway, cutlass drawn. William sat down immediately and sank back, out of the candlelight.

'I visit you as a riding officer of His Majesty's Customs...' the young man began, addressing the room without looking at anyone in particular.

'We know who you are, Mathew Allen,' said Elizabeth. 'You search our house almost every week, and you always find nothing.'

The man waved his cutlass in a way that was probably supposed to be threatening. William would have laughed at him, but this was not a good time for the customs to call.

'Well,' said Allen, 'somebody is smuggling fleeces out of England. Somebody is selling brandy and tea.'

'Oh, great crimes indeed,' said Elizabeth, smiling. William edged into the darkness towards the door.

'And somebody is bringing French Jacobite traitors into England!'

'Well, it's not me,' replied Elizabeth. 'Please, feel free to look around.'

'I will!' said Allen, poking the air with his cutlass.

'Put it away, Mathew,' said Juliana curtly. He wheeled round.

'Mother?' He sheathed his cutlass instantly. 'What are you doing here?'

'They were just seeking my advice on a farming matter,' she said. 'Now do what you have to do and run along.'

'Right,' said Allen. William took advantage of the distraction and slipped out of the room.

Behind him, he heard his mother say, 'The only reason you bother us is because you're afraid to go after the real smugglers. You know who they are, sure enough. What are they paying you?'

It was true. The organised smugglers basically ran the coastline and the law couldn't stop them. But they were dangerous people. Mathew Allen was obviously under pressure to show he was doing something, but if he tried to take them on, he'd probably wind up dead. So instead he turned up at William's house every other week on the off chance of catching them with a couple of sacks of wool.

William would have felt sorry for him on any other day. But not today. Today he just hoped his mother could buy him enough time to get the woman out of the coal shed and up the hill into the tomb.

He could hear Allen crashing about in the bedrooms upstairs as he ducked outside and into the garden. He beckoned the woman out and grabbed her hand, keeping her low as they skirted the edge of the garden and slipped out towards the woods.

Once they were safely under cover of the trees, he stopped and straightened up. In the moonlight, she had a slightly odd-looking face. Pale and sharp. Sculpted down into a slender neck.

He realised he still had hold of her hand, and let go abruptly.

'They're searching the house,' he said. 'We have to go now.'

'Thank you. I know this is for you a risk,' she replied, softly.

This close to France, words and accents merged and mingled across the Channel, but her voice marked her out as having been on a much longer journey before she'd turned up on the Normandy coast, looking for safe passage to England.

'Life in France is not easy if you carry new ideas,' she went on. 'Perhaps it will be better here?'

'Perhaps.' William thought about the meeting he had just crept out of. He didn't think it would be easier at all.

'But your parliament now can overrule your king, no? You have Mr Isaac Newton. Your church, she cannot do just as she pleases.' She smiled. 'The way people think… it is changing.'

'It's not quite as simple as that,' he managed. It was true that the king and queen were invited to rule and more or less told how to do it by parliament nowadays. It was also true that the more people knew how to read, the more resistance there was to mindless unfairness. William felt proud to have played some small part in that himself, but he was all too aware how far his England was from the England those fleeing persecution in France imagined. The secret library was, after all, still secret. 'Things change slowly,' he said.

They made their way in silence up to the tomb. William loosened the stone at the top of the door and edged it out just enough to free the top three stones. He had done it so often he could open the tomb in the pitch dark and seal it again invisibly, but all the same he lit two lamps and gave one to his guest, gestured at her to descend and then followed her into the tomb.

When he reached the bottom of the steps, she was simply standing, staring. William deliberately never mentioned the tomb's occupant to his foreign guests as they passed through. He preferred to wait until they discovered the creature for themselves, and watch their eyes. Hers were bright. Searching. They seemed to pick over the skull, making a journey around the huge eye, and up along the jaw, flicking up to the point of each curved tooth in turn.

'What is it?' she whispered eventually.

'Don't you have dragons in France?' he said with a dismissive shrug. Then he added 'Oh, don't worry. There aren't many left now. Most of them have been argued to death by Mr Isaac Newton.'

She laughed.

William smiled back. Then he looked at the skull himself. She – ever since his father had first brought him here as a child, he had thought of the creature as 'She' – looked different today. William had always fancied that She had moods. That She watched what went on in her tomb and reacted to its visitors, to their stories and their plans.

When the young rebel with his demands for revolution had passed through, She had seemed to look right through him as though he was not even there. When the frantic preacher-philosopher had arrived, scribbling his notes as he tried to force his God into a set of rational rules, She had seemed almost amused by him. And on the night he learned that his father had been lost at sea, when the whole village bustled through the house, swamping him and his mother with sympathy, he had crept up to the tomb to be alone and found She had changed again. Suddenly closer to him. Part of his father, but somehow now part of him as well.

Today She was brooding as if with a dark thunder. Looking into her eye, William felt he was lost, pitching in a stormy sea.

He blinked and forced his eye back to his guest.

'But you're not here for that,' he said. 'This is what you want.' He took the lamp and led her over to the other side of the tomb.

Further back in the room stood shelves containing the books of the secret library. The ancient ones were beautiful, but were seldom read. It was the modern printed volumes, and more especially the thin, paper-bound pamphlets piled on the floor, that made it necessary for the library to stay secret. They were filled with dangerous ideas: treachery, heresy, philosophy, science. Behind the books was the most secret thing of all.

It was a large workbench with a tall, solid wooden frame halfway across it. Embedded within the frame was a heavy rectangular plate which could be lowered by pulling on a metal handle until it pressed hard into the surface of the bench. The entire structure was stained with printer's ink and beside it piles of fresh, unprinted paper lay waiting.

'Do you know how to use it?' William asked.

'Oh, yes,' said the woman quietly, running a hand down the side of the printing press as though she was steadying a horse. 'I know.'

William paused. 'I can stay and help for a while,' he said. 'If you like?'

The process was slow. William sat with the box of letters, each one embossed in reverse on its own metal peg, while the woman, Marie, held the block that would house them. As she called for letters one at a time, he found them in the box and handed them to her so that she could arrange them in neat rows. He knew it could be weeks before the block was ready to print the first copy of her pamphlet, but once it was made she would be able to run off hundreds, even thousands of copies in a day, ready to take with her when she left.

'Another *s*,' she said. He handed it to her. 'And a *c*.'

'It must be dangerous,' he said, nodding at the block on her lap. 'This idea.'

Whatever her pamphlet was about, it had resulted in her being hounded out of France and fleeing across the Channel in a boat never meant for the journey.

She looked up from her work. 'Oh, yes,' she said. 'It is the most dangerous idea in the world. An *i* please.'

He handed it to her. 'Tell me,' he said.

'Truth,' she began, starting to press letters into the block, 'is like water in your hands. If you leave gaps in your thinking, it just trickles away, and you are left with nothing. You must be rigorous – rigorous in your thinking. In your investigation of the world.

Look here.' She picked up her lamp and placed it on the press. Its flame burned brightly. 'Suppose I covered the hole in this lamp. What would happen?'

'It would go out,' he said.

'Of course. You know that.'

'Yes, it's obvious.'

'But how do you prove it? How do you make it such a truth that it cannot be disputed?'

'I cover the hole,' he said simply, 'and the lamp goes out.'

'Ah, but that is not enough,' Marie said. 'Then I can argue. I can say perhaps the lamp just ran out of oil. Perhaps there was water in the lamp. Perhaps the wick was at fault. Do you see? The truth – it trickles away like water.'

He opened his mouth to object, and then shut it again. 'Then how do I prove it?'

She reached over and placed his oil lamp next to hers on the bench. The flames flickered together. 'This other lamp. It was filled at the same time, yes?'

'Yes.'

'And it was lit at the same time. I saw that,' she said. 'And it is stored in the same place?'

'Yes.'

'The wick is from the same rope? The oil from

the same source? They are the same size? The same shape? The same craftsman made them in the same workshop?'

'I bought them together,' he said.

'Then they are the same.'

'Yes, but – '

She held up her hand to signal his silence, and covered the holes in her lamp with her palm. The flame flickered and died. 'So now, we have held all other things the same. We have control of every part of our experiment and we have changed just one thing.' She smiled triumphantly.

'So?' said William.

'So you cannot now blame the wick, yes? You cannot blame the oil or the lamp or suggest it was an older lamp or a newer one, or that the lamp went out because I had somehow treated it differently. You cannot avoid the truth. It does not trickle away. It stays in your hand.' She sat back in the light of the single flame still burning. 'That is rigour.'

'It doesn't sound very dangerous to me,' he said.

'That depends on how it is applied,' she said darkly. 'If you can find a truth and not just know it but show it and prove it to be true – no gaps – if you can do that then nobody can argue that you are wrong.' She paused. 'Not a judge. Not a king. Not a god. You see now how this is dangerous?'

William nodded. On his back, he felt a hot draft as though the creature in the wall was breathing, but when he turned, he saw it was the first light of the sun shining into the tomb.

Elizabeth was waiting for him when he got home. She was sitting at the head of the table. She might have been there since he'd sneaked out of the room. In front of her, the little idol was standing on the table surrounded by seeds, just as he'd left it.

'You're going to have to go to France again and bring back the cart,' she said.

'What?' She didn't believe this nonsense about the idol, surely.

'Juliana knows everything.'

'She thinks she does...' he started. Then he saw the expression on his mother's face. She wasn't talking about blessings and curses.

'The boat. The tomb. The press. She knows everything.'

'And me going to France is – what?' He hesitated. 'Her price for not telling her son?'

Elizabeth nodded. 'I don't believe this blessing will work any more than you do. But we have to hope we're wrong. We have no choice.' She stood up. 'It'll take about three weeks to collect the money from everyone.' William could tell she was nearly in tears, but she just smiled tightly and left the room.

He stared down at the collection of objects in the centre of the table. He was full of fury. It was so clear to him. It was the seeds that would save the village, not the idol. He knew it. But he couldn't prove it. And as he stared, one word kept reappearing in his exhausted mind: rigour.

William had no idea how long he'd slept, but the moment he woke – still sitting at the table – he knew exactly what he had to do.

He grabbed the little idol from the table and a handful of the beans, tipping them into a pouch and tightening the drawstring. Then he went to the kitchen and took three small bowls from the dresser. Finally, he opened the sack containing the paler dried beans they'd managed to keep over from the last meagre harvest for sowing this year, and put a few into another pouch.

When he arrived at the tomb, Marie was curled up on the floor, sleeping next to the few paragraphs she had so far assembled of her pamphlet.

On the wall, the skull was crossed with rays of dusty light. She seemed stiller than usual, as if waiting for something.

'I need your help,' he heard himself say in a loud voice. 'I need to get this exactly right.' Marie stirred and sat up. William wondered if he had been talking to her, or Her.

Marie listened while he told the story of the last few years. The erratic weather, the failed harvests. The slow creep of desperation among the villagers, and with it the grasping for answers in superstition. It felt good to talk to someone who wasn't caught up in it. When he told her about last night's meeting, and its outcome, she understood his idea immediately.

'We must make everything the same,' she said. 'Everything. And just change one factor at a time.'

'No gaps.'

'No gaps.' She smiled.

On the floor just in front of the skull's huge eye socket, William laid out the three bowls. Each he filled with soil.

'The same soil?' she asked.

'Dug at the same time from the same part of the same garden,' he replied.

In the first bowl, he placed a sprinkling of the French seeds, which he carefully covered with earth. In the second bowl, he planted seeds from the family's own store. In the third bowl, he planted the same local seeds, but once they were covered, he took the tiny wooden idol from the pouch and planted it in the bowl beside them, turning its veiled face so that the spirit, or goddess, or whatever she was supposed to be, could look over the seedlings. Together, he and Marie measured out equal amounts of water and poured them into each bowl.

'There,' he said. 'Finished.'

'No,' Marie said. 'This is not good enough.'

William looked at the bowls. Everything was the same for each, surely. 'What?'

'Your witch. She said there was dancing, no?'

'Yes, but that's just foolishness.'

'No, no, no!' Marie shook her finger at him. 'It does not matter what you think. You must hold your friend to the same standards as your enemy. You must treat your beliefs as if they are as false as those you find foolish... until the experiment is over. Then you will know.'

'So...?'

'We must dance.' She held out a hand and he took it. 'I used to love this song when I was a girl,' she cried, and started to sing.

And there, under the gaze of the tiny idol and the giant stone eye, they danced. William was faltering and embarrassed at first, but Marie was confident, and as she showed him the steps, he gradually started to move to the rhythm of her voice. Soon, they were both stepping joyfully through the simple dance, spinning around, touching fingertips, stepping away from each other, and then suddenly close, and then away again. Once they stepped past each other, and he held her waist as she turned.

When she finished the song, they sat on the steps and giggled together like children. William felt it had been a long time since he'd laughed like that. Then Marie reached up through the gap in the tomb wall, picked a tiny flower from the overgrown roof of the tomb, and they solemnly placed it into the bowl in front of the little veiled lady.

For a moment, they were both quiet. The dancing. The singing. The solemn ritual. The sacrifice of the flower. It all seemed right somehow. Powerful. As if something warm and strong and good was seeping into the tomb. Perhaps there was something in it after all.

'Now, remember. Everything the same,' Marie said. 'The same sunshine. The same water. Every day. Everything the same. We will see the truth.'

William took the bowls home and placed them beside the sunniest window. All three were aligned to get the same amount of sun as it passed over. Each day, he fed the seeds with a carefully measured portion of water, always from the same source. Always at the same time of day.

Every day, William went to the villagers to collect whatever they had put aside for him to bargain with over the goddess in the cart. Whenever he could, he stole away to sit in the shadow of the stone skull and hand metal letters to his exile, hiding in the secret library.

Within a week, a single green sprout was rising above the soil in the pot containing the wooden idol. It curled upwards, pale, almost white at first, but growing stronger as it reached towards the light. A tiny leaf seemed to grow and unfurl as William watched. The idol was winning.

But by the tenth day, all three pots had sprouted, and by the time all the payments had been collected and the boat had been prepared to leave, the result of the experiment was clear. Two of the pots had modest crops of sprouts. Two or three shoots tentatively probed the air above their soil. But the third – the darker seeds from the French side of the Channel – were exploding. They had almost all germinated, and they brimmed over the top of the bowl, leaves spreading to hide the soil, jostling for the light like hungry chicks.

It was time to present his results. Not to the whole village this time. He spoke to Elizabeth, and she gathered a few farmers that she thought might listen, just before he was ready to leave for France. William had hoped to go up and say goodbye to Marie, to see if he could bring her back anything from her old country, but there was no time. At least he would only be gone for a few days.

The farmers sat quietly and listened while William explained what he had done. They were as suspicious, to begin with, as they had been before. The village was proud of its seeds, and when they sold their crop, it sold well because it had a reputation. A new seed was a big risk. But William spoke slowly and clearly, and when he had finished, he placed the three bowls next to each other on the table.

His audience leaned in. The green shoots told a story no one in the room could afford to ignore. William answered their questions one by one. Yes, they had had the same amount of water. Yes, the soil had been the same soil. Yes, they were planted together.

Elizabeth nodded at her son, almost smiling. It was going well. Then Old Jack, the quietest of the farmers, and the one who'd tended his land for the longest of all of them, slowly sucked his breath through his missing tooth, and nodded at the bowl containing the wooden statue.

Everyone turned to listen. He was no great friend to new ideas, and still dug with the lucky spade his grandfather had used. He was held in great respect by all the other farmers, and he knew the land inside and out. He smacked his lips thoughtfully.

'Tell me, son.' He spoke slowly and deliberately. William held his breath. What had he forgotten? What had he overlooked? Old Jack nodded at the idol again. 'Tell me, did you do the dance?'

William laughed as a wave of relief swept over him. He flushed slightly.

'Yes, Jack. I did the dance.'

'In that case, son, I'll take some of your seeds if you can get 'em.' He paused and then added sternly, 'But don't go getting any ideas. You'll bring us that statue too. It'll take more than a bowlful of sprouts to change most of their minds.'

CHAPTER 5

WILLIAM MARCHANT, 1693

It was a clear night as William and his mother pulled the little boat from its hiding place and pushed it into the water. He could feel her standing on the beach, watching him long after he lost sight of her in the darkness. The water was calm, but he knew she hated sending him alone, and would worry until he returned.

'The sea can turn,' she always warned him. 'It can turn so quickly!'

He knew he could handle himself on the water, but he didn't blame her for worrying. His father had been able to handle himself too, and the sea had still taken him.

There was enough wind for the sail, but he couldn't risk raising it, not until he was well out of sight of land. Night was a busy time at the shoreline. The game of hide-and-seek played out between the customs officers, the navy and the big smuggling gangs was barely less than a war. Either side would kill him before they asked who he was, and being a small, dark dot on a huge dark sea was the best defence he could hope for.

He dipped his oars silently into the sea, and pulled the tiny dory slowly and smoothly out towards deeper water.

The moment he passed the tall outcrop of cliffs that marked the end of the cove, he knew he was in trouble. He jammed his oars into the water and pushed hard to bring himself to a halt.

The naval lugger had its sails ready, but was barely moving. Not patrolling, not chasing, just waiting. For him? He didn't think so. It was a big, fast ship to send after a boy in what was little more than a rowing boat. But if they saw him, he'd have no chance. And the ship was very, very close. He could see the figures milling about on deck. He could see the buttons on their uniforms shining as it loomed out of the darkness above him.

He quickly and silently brought his boat around, and looked up at the sentries. They were scanning the horizon for smugglers' vessels. Luckily, nobody was looking straight down.

William thought quickly. If he could get back around the outcrop of rock without being spotted, he could loop around to the other side of the cove. By then he'd be too far away for his little boat to be seen.

Wincing at the sound each oar made and the noise of the water slapping against the hull, he rowed as quietly as he could back around the cliff. The moment he was out of sight of the naval lugger, he sunk his oars into the water again and rowed with all his might.

It was a race against time now. The ship was not in full sail, but it was catching some wind, and it would only be a few minutes before it rounded the cove and he came fully into its view. His boat had seats and oars for two more men, and was heavy enough to need them to get up any great speed, but on the way back, there would be no room for helpers, so he was on his own. His arms and legs burned with the effort as he raced the little boat across the cove.

Just as he reached the outlying rocks marking the boundary between the cove and the next beach along the coast, he saw the lugger's bow appear like a dark shadow. It was in sail and gaining speed.

What now? He pulled the boat around, and started into the next cove. Perhaps he could find somewhere to shelter until the ship had passed. But as he skirted the final rock, he realised his problems were much more serious.

Where the shallow waters of the cove shelved off into the deeper channel, another boat was waiting. Bigger than the revenue ship, and older. Patched, scratched, splintered, and painted black, with dark sails. He knew it well enough. It belonged to the Harkler gang, and you did not mess with the Harkler gang.

The ship was low in the water, and that meant it was full of cargo. That in turn, meant it had just arrived, so as well as the thirty or so smugglers on board who would be ready to kill him on sight, there would be another hundred or so on the beach or rowing cargo to and from the ship, ready to kill him if he tried to land.

William did the only thing he could do. He tested the wind, hauled up his tiny square sail, yanked it tight, and headed straight out to sea. The wind was not strong, but he caught it well and started to pick up speed.

The shout went up almost immediately. First from the big ship, then from somewhere in the water behind him. He squinted into the darkness where he could just make out a small rowing boat. The rower had arms like tree trunks, and the boat's bow lifted out of the water as it sped towards him.

He frantically dipped his oars in the water, adding his own strength to the power of the wind, and the boat picked up a little more speed. It would not be enough to pull his heavier boat away from his pursuers, but it didn't need to be. He just had to stay alive until the smugglers and the navy encountered each other and he could slip away from them both.

He heard a shot from the big ship, and a hole punctured his sail. He ducked, but carried on rowing. The tub-boat was gaining on him now, and he could see the rower clearly. A huge, heavy-set man with a bald head that seemed to be nothing but a growth on the heaving muscles of his shoulders. To his left, the smugglers were running to the side of their ship. He could see them shouting and pointing at him. Those with guns were aiming them. Those without were signalling his position to the other tub-boats.

Away to his right, where the smugglers still could not see, the naval ship had also spotted his sails and was in full chase. It would be on him in seconds. Against all his instincts, he steered left towards the gunfire. It had the effect he wanted, and as the shots seared into the water around him, the big rower in the tug-boat lost his nerve and broke off the chase.

William turned back to the right, rowing hard and trying to get back out of range of the guns. They were firing randomly and in the dark, so as he headed away from the coast, he tried to keep his range from the big ship constant – just far enough that the chances of being hit were slim, just close enough that the swarm of little rowing boats now shadowing him would fear being hit themselves. It was a dangerous game, and he was running out of time.

Suddenly, all hell broke loose. The navy lugger reared out from the cover of the cove. The smugglers started to reload in panic as a crack of simultaneous gunfire erupted at them from the navy ship. The rowing boats were scattering as their occupants headed for land, sea, or just out of the way of the speeding ship.

The naval ship itself was also changing direction. William realised with relief that it was no longer chasing him but was turning to take the Harklers' vessel head on.

As the wind grew in his sails, the sounds of shouts and gunfire gradually died away behind him. There would be a battle tonight, but he would not be part of it.

Eventually he could see no land in any direction and hear nothing but the sea. The stars were bright in the sky, and their reflections twinkled in the sea so that he almost felt as though he was drifting among them. His destination might as well have been Mars.

The wind was good, and the weather calm, but it took all night and all the following day before he caught sight of the French coast. He knew the beaches well and had a good idea where he could bring the little boat in, hiding it among rocky outcrops protected from view from the sea or the shore. To be on the safe side he waited for dusk and high tide before slipping in to shore, securing his boat, curling up in the bottom of the hull and finally collapsing into sleep.

This wasn't going to be easy. The cart with its idol was important to the locals and William didn't think that putting it on a boat and taking it out of the country, however briefly, would go down well with most of the people he did business with. The one trader who might be able to help was not someone he enjoyed meeting.

He kept off the main street and put his head down as he slipped into town, circling around behind a shabby row of cottages to De Cuir's back door.

The fewer people who knew he was in town, the better. If things went wrong, they could go very wrong indeed, and William's ability to trade here in France was the only thing keeping him and Elizabeth fed.

De Cuir's home was dark and shabby, just like the man himself. He was thin, sour and unshaven. As he ushered William in, his eyes darted along the street to make sure nobody had seen the Englishman enter, and he closed the door quickly behind them.

Most of the people William dealt with in France were not criminals. At least, not real ones. They didn't ask much about where the fleeces he sold came from, or where the brandy and tea he bought in exchange went. Like the farmers back home, they were not well off enough to refuse a good bargain, and they saw nothing wrong in striking one. Trade across the Channel was a way of life. Illegal and dangerous, but a way of life nevertheless.

De Cuir was different. He charged high prices and would rip you off if he got half a chance. But he could get you *anything*. Whatever you needed, somehow, somewhere, he would know someone who could lay their hands on it, if the price was right.

William sat on a hard chair in his back room, and explained exactly what he needed. The idol, the cart and the seeds. De Cuir listened, drumming his fingers against each other. William could see his narrow eyes darting from side to side, but his expression did not change.

When William finished De Cuir laughed dryly, without smiling. 'Your crops aren't growing so well, are they?'

William didn't answer that. 'Can you get me what I need?'

'The beans I can bring you. They are no problem. This charm... There is only one Lady of the cart. She travels from one village to the next. The farmers, they make an offering to the Lady – and another to the cart driver. Then he goes away, and returns next year. It is a... a service.' De Cuir waved his hand. 'He follows the season of sowing. You see?'

'You mean you cannot get it?' said William.

'I did not say that. The weather, it is not so honest with us this year. In the South, it has been warm early – the seeds have been planted. The Lady, she has finished her work, and come early to town.' He paused. 'But we… we are still too cold for planting. We have storms. The lady cannot do her work for two – three weeks yet.'

William smiled. 'You mean it's here?'

'Possibly,' said De Cuir vaguely. 'There would be a price.'

'Of course.' William explained what money he had and that there was no way to negotiate – he could get no more. De Cuir looked disappointed, but William could tell he wasn't really. 'That's all I have. We can make a deal, or not.' William shrugged.

The Frenchman nodded. 'The driver keeps her in a barn, and stays in town enjoying free food, wine and friendship wherever he goes.' He pulled his lips tight, in what probably passed for a smile. 'He would not notice if she went on a trip for a couple of weeks.' He suddenly grabbed William's wrist. His hand felt like an iron cuff. 'But no more! For some reason, people look to me when things go missing here. I don't want questions. You understand?'

'So you can get it?'

'Me? I will have nothing to do with this.' De Cuir paused. 'The cart is built to be pulled by two heifers. I will leave two for you at our usual place, and I will tell you where to find the cart. Anything you do will be your own decision. I want to know nothing more about it. You will give me half the money now, and leave the heifers and the rest of the money at the beach, where I will leave the seeds.' He held out his hand.

William reluctantly handed over half of the money and De Cuir almost bundled him out of the house, checking up and down the street to make sure they hadn't been seen before slamming the door shut behind him.

The barn was just a shed, and its roof was sagging, but there was no lock and no other building close by. William approached cautiously, leading the two mooing heifers DeCuir had left for him, but he soon realised that the Frenchman had been right – the barn was in the middle of nowhere. Until sowing started, nobody was going to make the journey out here to check on the idol in the cart. Certainly, at midnight, he felt sure he'd be undisturbed.

Inside, he lit a lamp and, sure enough, a little cart stood in the corner. The base of the wagon was old, very old. But its wheels had been replaced with new ones, several times by the look of their fixings. The cart itself had had rough sacks thrown over it to protect it from bat droppings. He grabbed them and pulled them away. Underneath, a full-sized wooden carving of a lady was built into the wagon as though it was a chair.

She sat bolt upright at the centre of the wagon, swathed in a deep blue gown and stared straight out towards William. At least, that was what he felt as though she was doing. He couldn't tell in reality, because her face was completely hidden by a carved veil. Secured by twine, the wooden veil covered both the front and back of her head. In one hand she held a sheaf of wheat, and in the cart around her, carvings of fruit and vegetables were garishly painted. The decoration spilled over onto the sides of the cart where painted and carved leaves and berries intertwined with flowers and ears of corn.

It was quite a piece of work. Bright, colourful and imposing. Wherever he tried to look, William's eyes were drawn up to the veil hanging in wooden folds over the goddess' head. He knew, of course that it was solid wood, that there was no face behind the veil, and yet he felt as though there were eyes behind. He felt as though she was looking down. Watching him hook the cart to the two animals.

There would probably have been room for William to sit on the goddess' lap and drive the cart, but somehow he couldn't bring himself to sit on her. The animals didn't complain as he led them off.

The cart track was empty all the way back to the fork where it joined the main road to town. William put out his lamp and covered the Lady with the sacks as he headed on, but he knew he'd still be a fairly odd sight leading two heifers pulling a wagon at this time of night. He only had to stay on the road until it forked again and he could take the fishermen's route down to the beach, but it felt terribly vulnerable.

He could see the outlying houses of the town just a field away. Some still had lamps at their windows, and he could see shapes moving about inside. If anyone looked out, they might see a shadow on the road and think it odd enough to come out and check.

The animals were well enough behaved, but heifers were not quiet by nature. As he passed close to the wall of the nearest house, one of them let out a long moan. William froze to the spot. If anyone had heard, then the game was up. Anyone hearing a cow here would assume it had got loose and was munching through their vegetable store. They would be sure to run out after it. He held his breath.

Nobody came. He grabbed the reins and led the animals away as quickly and quietly as he could, down the little rough track away from town and towards the beach.

He'd only gone a little way when he suddenly heard a shout up ahead, and then another. Someone was coming. He looked around frantically. The ground was flattening out on to sand dunes. Maybe, if he could get the cart off the track quickly enough, and if whoever was coming kept their eyes on the path...

It was a huge risk, but it was the only chance he had. He tugged on the reins, and the creatures tugged back. They wouldn't move. He pulled again, harder this time, but the animal closest to him just tossed its head. He yanked with all his strength, but it was too late.

Three figures stepped out of the darkness in front of him. They were fishermen – he could tell by their dress – and they were walking straight towards him. One was carrying something heavy-looking in one hand. He swayed a little as he walked, and his friend steadied him.

As the three men stopped in front of him and slowly looked his cart up and down, William saw the man was carrying a bottle. This could get ugly. He looked around for the best direction to run.

The three men didn't say anything for a few moments, then the man at the front leant forward to William and slapped him on the shoulder.

'Bonsoir!' he said in a loud voice.

'Bonsoir,' William replied cautiously.

'Bonsoir!' the others chorused. The three men smiled broadly and staggered on past him. They were so drunk they could barely stand. William thought they probably didn't see anything odd about him driving his cart to the beach in the early hours. If they remembered it at all tomorrow, they'd never recall what he looked like, or guess what was under the sacking in the back of the cart.

He hurried on to where the sand dunes widened out to the shoreline. There was plenty of cover here, but he would have to work fast. He secured the animals and ran off up the beach to where his boat was hidden. It was a twenty-minute run to where the sand gave way to broken rocks, before he could wade out into the icy water and around a jutting cliff to the secret place where the boat was hidden.

Once he'd retrieved it and dragged it back into the water, he rowed as hard as he could to bring it back down to the sand where he could load it. He grounded it on the beach and used a couple of planks of wood to form a makeshift ramp from the sand up into the boat.

William led the two animals down into the water and released them from the cart. He would have to get it on to the boat by himself. He pulled it around to line the wheels up with his ramp. He was already worn out from the walk, the run and the rowing. It wasn't an easy job.

The cart was a small one and didn't really need two animals to pull it, but for one young man alone it was a struggle to manoeuvre it up the ramp and into the boat. Each time he inched the wheels out of the sand and on to the wooden planks, it would slip back or jolt off the side of the ramp. But he kept trying and eventually managed to get the wheels over the side of the boat. The cart dropped suddenly into the hull with a sharp crack, but luckily neither the cart nor the boat suffered any significant damage. William stood back to assess his efforts. The cart was sitting high in the boat. The shafts stuck out to one side. This would never work. He would have to turn it.

He grabbed hold of one of the shafts and pushed the cart around, edging it a little at a time until the shafts faced along the length of the boat. He tipped them down and they fitted almost perfectly, locking in to each side of the boat in the stern and leaving just enough room for him and the oars and mast. It was precarious, but it fitted.

Quickly, he led the animals back to the place De Cuir had set for the exchange. The seeds were there, in several large sacks. De Cuir had kept his side of the bargain. William left the heifers and the money and dragged the sacks back to the boat, piling them into the bow to give the craft some balance for its top-heavy load. The sun was almost rising now. It was time to leave.

He heaved the little boat back into the sea and climbed in. It was sitting very low in the water. Dangerously low. The Lady in her veil pitched from side to side, towering above him as he rowed out to sea. The tiny boat rocked unpredictably in the ripples.

Going was slow. The Lady blocked most of the wind from the sails, and France seemed to take forever to disappear from view behind them. Once it was finally gone, the wind picked up, and they started to move faster, but with the wind came waves.

By nightfall, William knew he was in serious danger. He had watched and felt the storm coming in with slowly rising fear, and now it was all around him, pulling, rocking and tipping the boat from side to side. The sky was dark and the sea was a rolling, sickening landscape of heaving mountains, rising, falling and erupting around him.

His little boat was a solid design. It was long and deep, which meant it could hold a lot more cargo than one would expect of such a small vessel. It was easy to turn, and it was double-ended, so that if he really had to, he could swap around in his seat and start going backwards to make a quick manoeuvre. It was also flat-bottomed, so although it rocked enough in small waves to alarm anyone not used to sailing, it only would tip so far and no further – meaning that it was deceptively stable, even in moderately rough seas like these.

The problem with a deep, flat boat was that if the waves really did get up then it wouldn't tip or capsize. It would simply fill with water and go straight to the bottom.

All William could do was watch the waves, and fight to keep his little vessel angled straight into the worst of them so that it would ride them instead of taking their full smashing, tipping force against its sides, and hope to stay afloat until it was over. It was a constant and exhausting fight, and with every passing minute, it got harder.

The wind was strong now, and rain was slapping against the sail in rattling waves as the gusts changed direction. Looking up, a fork of lightning outlined the figure of Juliana's Lady, rising in front of him as though rearing out of the water. Her unseen eyes seemed to stare through the veil into his.

Out in the dark, heaving fury of the water, it seemed to William that a power was rising. It was the same power he felt when he looked into the huge empty eye socket in the tomb. A raw, natural power that was the force behind the storm, the force that turned seasons, that grew the crops or ruined them.

And it was in Her, too, the monster in the tomb.

Nature, in all its cruel glory, had taken his father. It did not care about William, his little boat or even the whole village. Human desires meant nothing to it. That much he had learned from Marie. He would cling on or he would not, and the storm would roll on regardless until it ended.

He dipped the boat into another wave so wide and high it blocked out the sky until it carried him up above the boiling landscape. For a moment, in the rolling waves under him, he thought he caught a glimpse of Her huge eye, not empty now, but alive, ringed with dark scales, Her curved teeth open and waiting, hanging just below the surface. This wild, tearing fury was Her world. Her storm.

Then suddenly, he felt the boat tip forwards and they were ploughing down the side of the wave, and into the next rising eruption, the oars twisting and dragging as William fought to keep his top-heavy boat upright.

He was weighing the choice in his mind before he even knew he would have to make it. He looked at the heavy sacks of seed in the bottom of the boat. He could almost feel them dragging him down, making every turn harder, slower. He felt the swell rise again at the front of the boat and pulled hard to turn in to the wave, over it and down and back for the next wave.

Then he looked up to the Lady above him. She towered against the sky, glaring down at him from behind her veil. The sheaf of corn looked like a club now, poised to strike him as she rocked back and forth with every pitch of the boat.

The choice churned in his mind like the boiling waves, without him being aware of it, until a huge heaving mound of sea struck at the side of the boat, sending icy water brimming over the side and into the hull, and he realised he'd known he would have to decide ever since he'd seen how low the boat hung in the water as he'd paddled out from the French shore.

It was clear now, but a long way from simple. His tiny boat held two cargoes. One weighed him down, the other pitched and tipped him from side to side. He could not carry them both to England. If he was going to stand a chance of making it to the shore alive, one of his precious cargoes would have to go.

He fought the notion. Perhaps if he just kept turning in to the waves... He turned again and paddled hard up and through a steep swell. At the top, the boat tipped and crashed, rocking into the next wave. A wall of water struck him hard across the back, bending him forwards over the oars. His frozen hands barely had time to steady the boat before another wave crashed down on him. There was water all around his feet now.

No good. The choice was there, stark and icy. The seeds or the idol. If he returned without Juliana's Lady, the consequences didn't bear thinking about. The fields would not be blessed. The village would see it as the worst possible insult to everything they believed in. They would surely turn against him and his mother. Everything would be in danger. Word would soon reach France of what he'd taken. He would never be able to return.

But if he abandoned the seeds to the ocean, the early crops would most likely fail again, and with nothing to sell, the village would be ruined. Within a year, the houses would be empty and those that survived would be forced to leave, to beg on the squalid, plague-ridden streets of London.

The icy water was numbing his skin. The oars burned in his hands as he hauled the boat around again to face another wave. He gritted his teeth and forced the muscles in his thighs and arms to pull again. He was gasping for air but he could only taste salt water splashing into his lungs, choking him.

A wave caught him side on, tipping the boat further and further over. The Lady's outstretched arm with its bundle of wheat scraped the water as the next wave pounded in. He was going over. He was certain of it.

A wall of water crashed down on him, and everything was chaos. He was spinning. He could feel the boat against his legs, the oars in his hands, and he held on because if he let go of either he was dead. The water covered him. For a moment he thought he'd capsized, but no, suddenly there was air again, and the

Lady was above him, white and ghost-like in a burst of blue-white lightning as she rocked and pitched.

He was still upright, but water slopped around his ankles, and the boat was lower in the water than ever. All his strength was draining from him. One more wave like that and it would be over. This was it. Now or never.

He felt the sacks of seed by his feet. They were soaked in salt water. Even if he got them home they might well be ruined. Above him, the Lady hovered, waving her bursting sheaf of wheat.

He felt the next wave building, sucking the water out from under the boat. It was a big one. The boat tipped backwards as William forced his aching arms to paddle hard up what felt like its sheer side.

They crested the wave, and already he could see the next one coming. It rushed at him, a huge dark monster rearing out of the darkness, foam tracing the shapes of scales across its wide arched back. In the second it took the boat to tip forward, he saw everything clearly, as if for the first time. He knew that monster would devour him when he reached the bottom, and as the boat pivoted, he made his choice. The seeds could be useless, but the Lady was definitely useless. He knew that. He had proved it. No arguments. No gaps. It was the truth, and here, now, at the top of this last wave, that was all that mattered.

He swung in both oars at the same time, and wedged them underneath the wheels of the cart. As he felt the boat start to fall, he jammed the oars against the sacks piled in front of him and pulled down with all his strength, levering them under the wheels.

The boat was in free-fall now, and gravity, for a split second was in retreat. As the cart started to tip he lifted both feet and braced them against the base of the cart. He pulled down as hard as he could with his arms and at the same time pushed with both legs. The cart shifted. Top-heavy, it tilted, and separated from the floor of the boat.

As the boat fell, William gave one last shove, and the cart toppled. Suddenly, they were two separate entities, plummeting down the side of the wave. He hit the bottom of the wave a fraction of a second ahead of the cart and brought his oars back into the water, digging them deep and pulling them around to greet the monster wave as it towered in front of him.

He ploughed into it, but with the cart gone, the little boat seemed to rise like a cork in the water, bobbing high on the back of the wave, rocking a little, but righting itself, almost immediately steady again.

William looked back. In the darkness, there was a shape. The cart's heavy wheels had pulled themselves downwards so that the base sunk below the surface, and now all that could be seen was the Lady, bolt upright and pale in the water, holding her wheat. Her veiled face stared out at William as she drifted into the darkness. Above, the wind was less fierce. The waves began to calm. Slowly, the storm was fading.

It must have looked as though he was dead, lying exhausted in the bottom of the boat, unable to find the strength to lift the oars or turn the sail. As soon as he saw the cove ahead and knew he was home, his body simply gave up, and he let the tide wash him slowly in towards the shore.

He knew he should wait offshore for the safety of night, but he wasn't sure he would make it to dusk. In the storm he'd lost all the food and small beer he'd brought for the journey. His legs and arms felt like useless lumps of meat. His throat burned with thirst.

As he felt the boat's hull softly nudge the beach, a shadow fell over his face and he opened his eyes to see his mother looking down at him. She pulled him up out of the boat and held him tight, stroking his head. She was almost crying with relief.

'I... I...' William rasped, barely able to speak. He waved an arm vaguely at the sacks in the bottom of the boat. 'The cart... I had to... I'm so sorry.'

'It's alright,' she said, hugging him closer. 'It doesn't matter.'

But it did matter. Even as Elizabeth held him, he could see Juliana over her shoulder, hurrying down the beach towards them. She stopped abruptly and looked down at the boat. Her lips tightened and her eyes narrowed with fury. 'Very well,' she spat, her voice a hiss. 'If your family no longer needs the help of my family, so be it.'

She turned and strode back towards the cliffs. William felt the darkness creep in around his eyes, and passed out.

'Quick! The old tomb!'

William was lying in his bed when the shout came through the front door and woke him. Beside him were the remains of a meal and an empty cup. His mother must have somehow got him home and given him food, though he had no memory of it. His eyes were hot with tiredness and his arms and legs still ached, but the shout brought him crashing back into consciousness. He rolled out of bed and scrambled to his feet.

The voice was one of the younger boys from the village, but as he opened the door, he realised it could have been anyone. The boy was already gone, running off towards the woods, and everyone else appeared to be running too, up the hill and towards the old tomb.

Elizabeth appeared in the doorway behind him.

'Go!' she cried. They ran together, William forcing his wobbly legs to propel him forwards through the crowd.

By the time they reached the tomb, most of the villagers were gathered around it. The stones in the doorway had been torn away and thick, dark, oily smoke was churning out of the hole.

Beside the doorway stood Mathew Allen, holding a burning torch and grinning like an idiot. Close to him stood his mother and a group of uniformed customs officers. One of them held the printing block from the press, its metal letters dark with ink, incriminating words written backwards across its face. Another two officers held Marie, ink-stained and fragile. She didn't struggle, she just stood, her neck stretched, holding her chin high.

Her eyes met William's and she acknowledged him without changing her expression. He started to step forward, but an arm grabbed his from behind. His mother. She silently shook her head. There was nothing William could do for her now.

He watched helplessly as the officers thrust yet more burning torches into the library, then gathered up the printing block and a few other scraps they'd taken as evidence. A moment later Mathew Allen, still grinning, made a grand gesture to his fellow officers. William's eyes filled with tears as they led Marie away.

As the tomb burned, the crowd began to drift off home. Juliana watched the smoke rise, then looked over at Elizabeth. As she turned to walk into the woods, she leaned in and whispered, 'I told him where. But I didn't tell him *who*. I could have, Elizabeth, but I didn't. You should be thanking me.'

By the time William could bear to return to the tomb, the shoots of the newly planted beans were bursting out all across the fields. They were strong and green, and for the first time in a long while hope bloomed on the faces of the villagers, though nobody showed any sign of forgiving William for throwing the Lady into the sea.

Marie was gone, taken to London where the authorities were determined to make some kind of example of her. But she would fight hard, and the courts were not entirely without rigour. There was a chance at least she could make her case heard.

The fire left nothing of the books or the press. All that remained were pieces of twisted metal and pools of solidified lead. Only the stone was undamaged. The floor, the steps, the hewn bricks and the old skull staring, blackened, from the wall. William gazed into Her empty eye. It seemed vacant now, as if she was drifting in a deep long sleep.

He left Her and climbed out for the last time. Slowly, he gathered the bricks from the ground where they had been thrown, and one by one, he fitted them back into place, cleaning each to ensure a tight fit.

As he sealed the final brick, he packed the cracks with soft clay. In time it would harden, and the bricks would grow together, held by soil and roots. One day, he thought, the tomb would be opened again.

When She was ready.

That day seemed a long way off.

Chapter 6
Henry Marchant: 1898

As his father grabbed the long table and flung it over, ammonites, trilobites and fossils Henry Marchant didn't recognise flew into the air, raining down on to the sand around him. He ducked and dodged, while his father continued to bellow at the woman in the long grey dress.

The moment he had heard that the fossil lady had set up a makeshift stall on the beach, his father had stormed out of his church, bible in hand, and marched to the seafront to confront her. Charles Darwin and his new ideas about evolution, he had told Henry in no uncertain terms, were like an infection, a plague on mankind. Such Godless ideas were to be fought, wherever they took hold.

Henry had heard this same sermon hundreds of times. Whether muttered over the dinner table, droned to a pious audience in church or screamed over the seagulls, it was the same message: God created the world in seven days. Only God can create life, and only God can take it away. Fossils are nothing. Darwin is wrong.

His father was right, of course. Fossils couldn't be anything more than random marks in the rock. A couple of weeks ago a lecturer had visited Henry's school. He had brought a model with him, a replica of a creature that had been built in the gardens of the Crystal Palace in London. The man had sounded more like a circus ringmaster than an academic, and his model looked fanciful. The creature appeared to be a cross between a dragon and a cow, the kind of thing you might invent to entertain children. Yet the boys at school all talked about ancient monsters lying buried in the rocks, and now here was this lady in her long grey dress. She looked earnest, with an honest face.

While his father was distracted, Henry picked up one of the small round stones and slipped it quietly into his pocket. He ran a finger around the spiralling, ridged impression inside the rock. It felt regular and measured. Not at all random.

Without warning, his father turned on his heel and stormed off along the beach, cassock flapping behind him. Henry turned to follow. A hand caught his; it was the woman with the long grey dress. She smiled at him and pressed a printed pamphlet into his hands. At the top, it read, 'The Dinosaurs of England'. Henry paused for a moment, then pushed the papers deep into his pocket and hurried off to catch up with his father.

The leather-bound books lining the dining room walls rarely left their shelves, but they sucked in light and sound. Dinner was dark and quiet, and Henry winced at the sound of his cutlery scraping against the china plate. His mother sat like a mouse at one side of the table, while his father, locked impenetrably in his own thoughts, sat at the other. Henry thought his father was capable of making silence the way other people made noise.

'I would like you to stay away from the beach,' Father said eventually.

Henry hated that thought. The beach was the one place he could go to escape the suffocating quiet of the house and the dead echoes of the church. At home, if you made the tiniest noise it would hang in the air forever. You couldn't tread on a stair or open a book without being heard and judged.

But the beach was a different place. At the beach, there was always sound. On a stormy day, the waves crashed against the rocks and the wind hammered the cliff and you could shout anything you wanted into it. On a calm day, the waves rattled back and forth over the pebbles, and it was as if the whole world was breathing, each exhalation carrying your secrets further out towards the horizon.

But there was no arguing with Father. You did what he told you to do, and you thought what he told you to think.

'Yes, Father,' Henry replied, staring at his plate.

'The world is changing, boy,' his father went on, sadly. 'Our nation is too rich and too much driven by engines. Today, it seems the best way to better your position is by publishing scientific papers. A man has to decide whether to look for his answers in the Bible, or to dig for them with his hands in the mud.' He paused, then said almost to himself, 'Only one thing lies down there, mark me.'

Henry didn't answer. He didn't really know what to say. He felt the round stone and the pamphlet still in his pocket and he couldn't look his father in the eye.

'Finish up,' said his mother after a long pause. 'It's time for bed.'

It was summer, and Henry's bedroom faced west, so even with the curtains closed there was plenty of light to read. He took out the stone and the papers from his pocket and quietly unfolded the pamphlet.

The type was small, crowding the page in solid blocks. It began by describing the differences between types of stone. It explained how one type of rock could only be laid down by layer upon layer of sand, and how another was made up entirely of crushed and rotted plant material. It detailed how a solid object – like a bone – might become a kind of mould in the forming stone so that when it finally did decay, it would be replaced by a completely different kind of rock to that which surrounded it.

Henry held up his tiny fossil in the dying sunlight streaming through the window. The stone itself was dark slate, but the perfectly coiled shell embedded in it was, indeed, entirely different. A smooth, shiny rock almost like crystal.

Henry turned it over and over in his fingers. The light seemed to glow through it. The pamphlet's explanation could not possibly be right, yet it seemed so obvious.

He read on. Now, the text described a few of the most sensational recent finds. A diagram of a bone caught his eye. Clearly it was a bone from an animal's lower leg – he was learning anatomy at school and the shape was unmistakable. Beside the diagram, an arrow indicated dimensions. The bone was huge. An animal with a leg that long could easily peer into his bedroom window.

'Megalosaurus: a giant predator', read the caption. Further down the page a curved, serrated tooth was pictured, as large, the text said, as a dagger.

The pamphlet described a ferocious monster stalking a distant jungle world, but the finds were well documented and their locations were listed. He recognised the names of villages and towns, all within a few miles of his home. One tail-bone had even turned up on his local beach. This distant jungle was his country. His village! Henry folded the leaflet and put it under his pillow along with the so-called fossil. He laid his head down, watching as the sun vanished and the shadows grew across his window, and fell slowly asleep.

* * *

Henry walked close behind his mother through the woods. She was usually so quiet and small, but now she seemed huge, purposeful. It was all Henry could do to keep up as he dodged through the ferns, stepping in the deep footprints she left in the mud.

She stopped suddenly, frozen, facing straight ahead. Henry looked up at her, wondering what she was looking at. He could see nothing in the trees ahead. She seemed to be listening, then she sniffed the air, turned and strode away into the forest. Henry followed, running after her. He felt the mud oozing between his toes, and the ferns scratching at his legs. It didn't feel cold.

It was a dark night but he could see well enough, and the trees were alive with noise. He caught up with his mother again as she stopped at the edge of a clearing. He ducked under her huge tail and stepped up beside her.

Breathing as quietly as he could, he looked out between the tree trunks. On the other side of the clearing, four camptosaurs were feeding. The two smallest were hunched over on all fours, grazing on ferns. The other two, the adults, were leaning back and stretching up to grab the tips of branches in their beak-like mouths, grinding them slowly from side to side.

The male stopped feeding and turned. He swung his elegant head from left to right, searching the edge of the clearing as if he knew he was being watched. His forelimbs rose in a defensive pose, hanging forward like a boxer's, but in place of gloves, he had long, spiked thumbs ready to stab any attacker. The creature sniffed, listened for a moment, then turned back to grab another mouthful of leaves.

Henry looked at his mother, but she did not move. She simply turned her heavy, scaly head towards him, and then back to the clearing. The moonlight glinted on her teeth. This was to be his first hunt.

He shifted his weight from one foot to the other, and jerked his head back to focus on the camptosaur group. The adults were too large, and he could not hope to bring them down, but the youngsters were about his size, and with their heads deep in the ferns at ground level they were less alert to danger.

He took a cautious step forward, poking his head into the clearing. Instantly, the big male swung around to face him. Both adults began to bay wildly and swing their thumb spikes threateningly, and the two youngsters ran and cowered behind them.

With the element of surprise gone, a more experienced hunter would have known to give up any hope of a kill. But Henry was not an experienced hunter. He launched himself into the clearing, snapping his jaws, then ducked as a thumb spike hooked over his head and had to leap to the side to avoid the male's massive tail.

Realising the danger he was in, Henry tried to turn and run back to the safety of the woods. But the two giants stepped forward to block his way, cornering him in an area of the clearing where the thick tree trunks made escape impossible. He backed up and opened his mouth as threateningly as he could, but on their back legs, the adults were twice his height and five times his weight. The male reared up and twisted his body, ready to bring down his spiked thumbs in a crushing blow.

There was a deafening bellow as his mother broke cover behind the two camptosaurs. Immediately, they lumbered around to face the new attacker standing between them and their young. On the other side of the clearing, the two youngsters leapt back in surprise and fled into the woods.

The camptosaur adults squared up to Henry's mother. Although she could easily bring down either of them alone, together they formed a fearsome wall of muscle and bone, four spiked thumbs swinging dangerously and unpredictably in front of them.

Behind them, Henry kept his distance from the swinging tails, watching his mother between the giants' flanks. He saw her snap her jaws at one, then the other, then draw back, studying their movements for a sign of weakness, or a gap between the flailing limbs.

He watched her rear up and take a step forwards, jabbing with her own front claw. As the male swung his body to fend off the blow she flung out the razor-sharp talons of her other arm, carving a deep gash into his shoulder. The male recoiled, while the female camptosaur brought her own claw up, slicing through the air a whisker away from his mother's soft throat.

Henry scanned the perimeter of the clearing for a spot where the trees were thinner, and edged sideways. The camptosaurs didn't seem to notice. The male was fighting one-handed now, but had turned slightly, so that his great tail was ready to swing. Henry's mother eyed it warily. One blow could knock her over or break her leg. She followed its movement, waiting for the right moment to attack, mouth wide open, ready to strike.

Henry saw his chance and broke for the edge of the clearing. The whip-like end of the female's tail caught him across the side of the head as he ducked underneath it, but he kept running and she didn't seem to notice. He heard a loud roar and a crash from behind him, but he didn't stop or turn. He simply dodged between the trees and kept running until the sounds of the fight disappeared into the background noise of buzzing and chirping insects.

Finally, he stopped. The trees were dark, but the smells were heavy and deep. Instinctively, his mind began to untangle them, separating one from another, sorting plant from animal, water from rock, building himself a picture of the jungle he could not see. He stood motionless, his tail rigid, balancing his body, his head low but alert. His claws clenched and unclenched slowly. Underneath the forest's smell was another scent. It drifted through the trees towards him.

It was the smell of prey.

He listened, trying to isolate his target among the forest's sounds and smells, tuning out the insects and rotting plants and the rustling of the leaves in the high branches. Suddenly, there it was – a low baleful moan, the unmistakable sound of distress. A young camptosaur. It must be one of the youngsters that had fled into the forest. And now it was alone, lost and vulnerable. It was calling for its mother, but its mother would not be coming.

He ran silently towards the sound, his feet deftly picking their way between fallen branches. Soon he saw it through the trees. The young camptosaur was tired and slowing down, wailing out its long, low cries. He knew he would have to act fast or he would not be the only predator determined to make this kill. His heart surged and he felt his body fill with a strange fury.

Without pausing, he ran straight at the camptosaur and leapt. The claws of both arms sunk deep into its back and he brought down his open mouth hard on the back of the creature's fleshy neck. It was over in seconds. The camptosaur gave a strangled cry and dropped to the ground as though its legs had suddenly lost all their strength. He held on tightly until there was no movement left and his prey's heavy chest sank for the last time as its final breath rattled from its lungs.

He fed quickly and greedily, swallowing chunks of raw meat. The smell of the kill would soon attract scavengers and many would be larger than him. After every mouthful, he raised his head to listen and sniff the air before sinking his head back into the carcass to tear off another chunk of flesh.

By the time the first light of the sun began to show through the trees, dappling the ground with orange streaks of light, he had eaten his fill. He left the dead camptosaur to be picked clean by ants, flying scavengers and the tiny feathered dinosaurs that roamed the forest floor. He crept into a thicket to rest, but his ears remained sharply tuned to the sounds of the jungle. Slowly, he became aware that below the humming and squawking of the Jurassic dawn chorus, something else was coming his way. Heavy feet were being placed one in front of the other with the practised care of a predator.

He shifted his position slightly and raised his head so that he could look out over the tops of the ferns without being seen. Between the trees he could see a large, dark shape: a great head, sharp claws and a long, solid tail. It moved slowly closer, the head swinging slowly left and right.

It was his mother. She was searching for him.

His first thought was to run to her side. He took a step, then paused. From deep within him, another instinct was rising. He had watched her hunt, and shared her kills, but now that time had passed. Today he had killed. Now he was a predator too.

He watched from the ferns as her huge bulk moved past, her teeth still glistening with blood. Her sharp eyes scanned the forest but did not see him. Her tail swung slowly from side to side as she passed on into the darkness.

CHAPTER 7

HENRY MARCHANT 1898

The sharp rays of the rising sun pierced through Henry's eyelids and into his dream, waking him suddenly. He felt cold. Cold and uncomfortable.

He opened his eyes. A vertical strip of sunlight framed solid blackness and he blinked, waiting for his eyes to adjust. Waiting to see the outline of the heavy curtains, the window. His bedroom.

His feet were freezing. He reached down to touch them and his hand recoiled. They were caked with mud.

A sick feeling grew in his stomach. His heart began to pound. He had walked in his sleep before, but he had never left the house. What had he done? Where had he been?

His hand dropped to the mattress of his bed. It was as hard as stone. No, it *was* stone. He sat upright. He was not in his bedroom.

His eyes began to adjust to the light. One wall was stone, crumbling, dusted with ancient ash. The opposite wall was rock and earth. He was sitting on a rough stone floor, at the foot of a set of deep steps leading up to a solid stone doorway. But there was no door. Just a block of stone which had once sealed the entrance, but which was now leaning open, propped against a tree, leaving the hole through which he must have entered in his sleep.

This doorway was familiar to Henry. It was covered in moss. Strands of ivy hung on the outside like a curtain. The frame of the door was carved from long, thin solid blocks and decorated with carvings of strange creatures. Some were rough. Others were more intricate and detailed. It was as though many builders from different eras had been competing, carving over and around each other's work.

Henry knew this place well, at least the outside of it. It was the old tomb deep in the woods above the village. He and his school friends told stories about it. They had studied its odd patchwork of different types of stone and carvings, but it had always been sealed.

The stone in the doorway had rocked tantalisingly when they had pushed on it, but it had never tipped open. They had always been too frightened of what might lie inside to try any harder to break in.

But now the great stone was leaning outwards. And here was Henry. Inside.

There was something else, too.

Where the sun glanced across the wall of rock and earth, it cast long shadows, bringing every indentation and detail of the stone into sharp relief. Henry stared at it, unable to move.

The huge eye. The massive skull. The curved serrated teeth. It was hypnotic and terrible.

The tiny spiral of the fossilised shell had been enough to make him ask questions in his mind. It had cracked open a door and filled him with doubt. But this... This was too big. It left no room for doubt. What Henry felt now, surging under the fear and dread, was pure, confident certainty. And it changed everything.

His father was wrong, completely and utterly wrong. And the woman in the grey dress was right.

Henry climbed out of the tomb with his head spinning. Using all his strength, he tipped the stone back into place. It wobbled and rocked as it always had. Perhaps it had only ever needed a push in the right direction to topple it out of position.

Henry reverently draped the ivy back over the entrance and set off home in his nightclothes.

It was only just dawn and luckily there was nobody else about. As he made his way down towards the vicarage, he could see no lights on in the house. The back door was ajar – obviously that was how he had left it during his sleepwalk. He ran out of the trees, across the empty cart-track and into the garden.

Good. All the curtains were still tightly shut. But he knew his father sometimes rose early to sit and work in the dining room on the other side of the house. If he was up, Henry knew he would be in deep trouble. He slipped in through the door and closed it as quietly as he could. The hinge creaked and the latch clicked loudly.

Henry held his breath and listened, but the house was silent. Eventually he dared to move again, tiptoeing across the kitchen and peering around the hall door. His eyes went immediately to the dining room. The door was open, but the room was in darkness. The curtains were still closed. That meant his father was not yet up. He breathed again.

There were two ways back up to his room: the main stairs, which would take him right past his parents' bedroom door; or the back stairs, which would take him closer to his own door, but which were old, loose and noisy.

Henry decided on the back stairs. He closed his eyes for a second and tried to remember which steps were the troublemakers. The first was fine, the second and third creaked if you trod on the left-hand side. He stepped cautiously upwards. The next three steps were good and solid, but then, on the seventh, there was a creak on the right followed by a creak on the left of the next step... or was it the other way around?

Gently, he lowered his foot onto the left of the seventh step. No sound. He put his full weight on it and suddenly the stair let out a loud groan. He jumped back and waited for the sound of a door opening.

There was a long silence.

Henry tried again, this time stepping on the other side, and crept upwards. The final two steps were both completely loose. He would have to jump. He grasped the carved wooden pineapple at the top of the banister and pulled hard on it as he leapt, clearing both steps and landing with a muffled thud at the top of the stairs. He smiled to himself in satisfaction, but when he let go of the banister, it gave a loud crack as it shifted back into place.

Again, he waited, his eyes fixed on his parents' bedroom at the end of the hall. Just as he was about to move again, he heard the sound he had been dreading. The sound of bedsprings pinging, followed by a creak of floorboards. Then came footsteps padding across the room.

His bedroom door was only three paces away and it was wide open. He leapt towards it, landing in the middle of the hallway. Out of the corner of his eye, he could see his parents' door handle turning. Skidding across the polished floor, he raced through his own door. He almost closed it behind him, then spun around to grab the handle and twist, pushing the door silently into place and releasing the handle carefully so that the latch let out only the tiniest click.

In the moment before the door shut, Henry saw his father framed in the doorway at the far end of the corridor. But he was looking back into his own room, not out into the hall. Henry had made it.

Henry was dressed for school and at the breakfast table exactly on time. In fact, he had been awake and watching the clock ever since getting home. His father slowly buttered his toast, scraping the knife back and forth until the butter vanished into the bread. A plate of cold meat sat at the centre of the table on a decorated china plate. Henry and his mother were careful to refrain from taking any until Father had selected his slices of choice.

Henry just wanted the meal to end so that he could leave for school. His father paused and looked at him. Perhaps he sensed that something was wrong. Henry did his best to hold his father's gaze, but in the end he looked away. He was still afraid of him. Yet something *had* changed. Yesterday, he had believed everything his father said because he knew more than Henry about the nature of the world.

Today, Henry knew more. Nothing his father said could be taken as the only interpretation of truth again.

'The more I hear,' his father's voice floated across the table towards him, 'about that school of yours, the less I like it.' Henry felt an accusation in his tone, as if he were solely responsible for the school, its teaching methods and its attitude towards discipline. 'The government has done children no good with its meddling,' his father went on. 'You should know I am considering other options.'

Henry knew what that meant. It meant being sent away to St Mary's. The mere thought made him shiver. St Mary's was more terrifying than any dinosaur. His own school was strict enough, but he knew it was nothing compared to St Mary's. His friends' parents used St Mary's as a threat. One whisper of the name was enough to make a naughty child behave.

The children of St Mary's were silent, humourless and blank. He'd seen them in town, walking in rows, heads bowed. Every spark of character erased from them. It was said that on their way between lessons they marched in time, and even at meals, they sat in silence. St Mary's had only one purpose for its students. Every graduate, or at least every graduate that anyone talked about, had a single calling. Every pupil that served his full term joined the church.

Henry felt a strange fury rising in his stomach. He knew it would be pointless, but he had to speak. He opened his mouth with no idea what he was going to say, but something stopped him.

His father was looking straight past him, his expression changing. His eyes widened, and his mouth was agape in horror or anger. He slowly rose to his feet.

Henry turned and followed his father's gaze. He

was staring out into the back hallway, and there, clearly outlined on the polished wooden floor, were muddy prints of Henry's bare feet. Between them, fallen leaves and sticks were scattered.

'What is this?' Henry's father leapt up from the table, and strode over to the offending marks. Henry stammered, unable to speak.

His father's eyes traced the footprints on to the stairs and upwards. He threw an accusing glance back at Henry and then followed the trail up the stairs, meticulously picking up leaves and sticks as he went. He said nothing, but Henry felt as though his throat was being squeezed hard. He swallowed.

Behind him, he could hear the slosh of water. His mother was already silently scrubbing the floor.

Henry watched his father follow his footprints to the top of the stairs and across the hall into his bedroom. By the time Henry got to the door, his father was already bending over the bed. He cursed himself for leaving the muddy trail on his way in. With all the curtains closed and the house in darkness, he hadn't noticed the trail of muck behind him. But at least he knew the bed itself was clean. He hadn't got into it since he returned from the forest. He had the worst of it now.

Suddenly, his father bent forward, reaching down and into the bed. Henry's heart sank as his father took two objects from under the pillow and stood up, staring at them, his face reddening. Henry had been wrong: things were now a lot worse.

His father's hand shook as he held out the printed pamphlet and the tiny fossilised shell in front of Henry's face. He said nothing.

'I…' started Henry, but his father grabbed his arm and dragged him out of the room. His wrist hurt as he was hauled down the stairs and out through the kitchen into the garden. It was an effort to stop himself falling over as he stumbled across the garden to the woodshed.

Henry's father stopped abruptly at the door to the shed. Outside, logs for the fire were piled in neat stacks. In front of them, a wide flat stone lay on the ground. Henry used it to hold logs while he chopped them for the fire. Sometimes his father made him chop wood as a punishment, but not today. This was far more serious. His father released his arm, leaving him standing bewildered in front of the stone block, and stepped into the shed. He didn't dare move.

When his father emerged, he was holding a large, heavy hammer. Its handle was as long as Henry's arm.

He stood in front of him for a long time, hefting the iron head in both hands. Henry waited, shaking.

After a long pause, his father held the sledge-hammer out to him. Henry took it. It was so heavy he nearly dropped it on his foot. It was an effort to stand up straight, but he did, looking his father directly in the eye for the first time. He was as furious as Henry had ever seen him, but still he said nothing.

Henry's forearm ached under the weight of the hammer, but he refused to let his arm drop. The muscles began to burn with the strain. Eventually, his father bent down and placed something on the flat stone, then stood up again, holding Henry's eye with his own.

Slowly, Henry looked down. There, on the flat stone, lay the fossil shell. Its coiled ridges stood out in creamy white against the slate surrounding it. Henry lifted his eyes back to his father's. Again, he said nothing, instead nodding from the hammer to the fossil, and back to Henry. Then he stepped back, expectantly.

His meaning was clear enough and Henry knew there was nothing he could do but obey. He looked down at the delicate shape, took a deep breath and raised the hammer above his head. It was all he could do to lift it.

He paused, his arms shaking, swallowing back tears, then brought the hammer down hard. The fossil jumped on the stone slab, but it didn't break. He hauled the hammer up again and smashed it down.

This time, the stone cracked from end to end and the slate fell away in pieces. The tiny shell lay completely exposed for the first time in three hundred million years. A perfect geometric spiral. So detailed and beautiful it could have been alive. Henry almost expected to see the hair-thin tentacles of the ammonite within, curling out of the shell to haul it away.

He lifted the sledgehammer and put his full weight behind it. The shell splintered into a powder of glittering crystals.

Henry dropped the hammer and stood up, staring defiantly at his father through his tears. Still, his father said nothing. With a look of disdain he turned away, and headed back towards the house.

Henry spent the day at school barely listening to his teachers' droning repetitions. He thought about the shell and his dream and about the skull in the old tomb. Most of all, he thought about his father.

Something told him that his punishment was not over. Something had changed between them. Whatever he now did with his life, he would have to do it alone.

When he got home, his father was at the church and his mother was busy in the kitchen. But as soon as he entered the dining room, he noticed it. The writing desk was always scrupulously tidy, just as everything his father touched was scrupulously tidy. Every object had a proper place and nothing was ever moved unless it was being used. Even the blotting paper was cut into equally sized pieces and arranged in a neat pile, held down by a carved wooden paperweight inlaid with brass leaves.

Anything out of place immediately caught the eye, and today, a long, white envelope sat at an angle in the middle of the desk. It was addressed, in his father's writing, to the headmaster of St Mary's.

The letter was sealed, but Henry didn't need to read it. There was only one reason for his father to write to St Mary's. Henry was to be sent there. He turned, ran upstairs to his room and threw himself down on his bed, sobbing. This was it. Quite simply, it was the end of his life.

He cried until the sun started to fade, sliding in a golden-red ball towards the treetops. His mind took him out into the woods where his secret lay hidden in the old tomb. He thought of the savage world the dinosaur must have grown up in and wished he could have its nature. Its strength. What, he wondered, could a boy achieve if he had the courage of a dinosaur in this polite, slow-moving world? He would not achieve anything at St Mary's, that much was certain.

By the time he came down to dinner, his eyes were dry and his face was set in an emotionless mask. His father was still not home and would not be until late. His mother tried to make conversation about the day at school, but Henry responded as little as he could. She smiled at him once or twice. A calm, sympathetic sort of smile that worked for a bruised knee, but would do no good now. His mind was fixed and nothing could be allowed to change it.

When dinner was finished and cleared away, it was time for bed. Before going upstairs, Henry watched his mother gather up a handful of his clothes from the washing basket and pile them in the dining room. With his father out, she could settle to mending and altering them.

As she sat there, darning with an oil lamp beside her, he wanted to go to her. To tell her he wouldn't be needing his school clothes any more. But he didn't. Instead, he stood at the door, and said softly, 'Goodnight.' Then he turned, closed the dining room door and walked up the stairs.

When he reached the top, he opened his bedroom door, picked up the large leather bag he had already packed with a few of his toughest clothes and most precious belongings, and crept back down the stairs and out of the back door.

He crossed the garden and the road at a run, and then he was into the woods. A little further on, he met the path that led away from the village.

It was that easy.

As he walked, he thought to himself, *It was the right decision. I had no choice.* At any rate, it was his decision, and his alone. He knew that children younger than him had made their way in England. Besides, he was educated and willing to learn more. And London was just a week's walk away.

He shifted the weight of his bag to his other shoulder and walked on. He wouldn't be missed until morning and by then he would be miles away.

He followed the curve of the path up and over the hill. When he reached the top, he could see out over the downs in the blue moonlight. He turned to look back down into the closed valley that had been his life, and for the first time, he felt free.

CHAPTER 8

STANLEY MARCHANT: 1932

'That's extraordinary!'

Stanley Marchant's geography teacher, Mr Grantham, was standing in their dining room, sloshing whiskey around his glass. Smoke was drifting up from a thin black cigarette dangling from his lip and Stanley didn't like it one bit.

Ever since Stanley had mentioned the picture to Herbert, Mr Grantham's son, his teacher had become uncomfortably chummy. Now he had brought Herbert over, using their friendship as a pretext to find out more about his father. Stanley knew this because the friendship between himself and Herbert was weak at best. They shared a desk, that was all.

Herbert was interested in nothing. Right now,

he was taking the carefully arranged bolts out of Stanley's Meccano set one by one and flicking them idly around the room.

Stanley turned his attention back to his father and Mr Grantham.

'And you say you've never been back in all these years, Henry?'

Henry Marchant took a sip from his drink and then stared deep into it. His son thought he looked sad.

'Never quite had the nerve.' He looked at the picture, then gestured at Stanley. 'I was barely more than his age when I left home that night.' He paused. 'My father had the best intentions for me, of that I have no doubt. But intentions are not always enough.'

'But you know exactly where it is?' Mr Grantham's voice was casual, but his eyes were gleaming.

'Oh, yes, I should say. I did live there my whole childhood, you know.' Henry reeled off the address of the vicarage where he had lived as a child. 'The tomb is well enough known in the village – although its contents are not.'

'And this picture? It's exactly what you saw?'

'On the morning after I ran away, I sketched it. It's not the world's greatest work of art, but I fancy I've an eye for detail. And it made quite an impression on me.' Henry laughed a little, but he looked slightly uncomfortable.

The picture had been on the wall in Stanley's house for as long as he could remember. It was a pencil drawing, outlined in ink, washed over with faded watercolours. The paper had been rolled, creased and torn. It had been with his father through a difficult time in his life, and contained the stains of the mud of four counties, and the dirt, soot and oil of a dozen dirty jobs. Now, it was framed and safe, and his father was standing beside it in a pressed suit.

At the top of the picture was a rough drawing of an old, ruined tomb. It was overgrown with ivy and blocking its doorway was a slab of stone, carved with shapes that Stanley could not make out. Below this image was another drawing. A detailed sketch of the skull of a dinosaur with a huge, empty eye-socket and a blunt mouth filled with curved, serrated teeth. The label underneath read simply: 'Megalosaurus'.

Stanley had always felt there was something strange about the sketch. He could not help but look at it every time he entered the room. It seemed somehow alive, as though the creature's great eye was staring at him through time. It had been watching him from the wall since the day he was born. It was familiar, but monstrous. The skull frightened him and drew him in at the same time.

'So it's still just sitting there, waiting to be dug up?' said Mr Grantham with poorly disguised excitement.

'As far as I know,' said Henry. 'If it had been found, I'm sure it would be in the British Museum. That's where it should be.'

'Possibly, possibly,' said Mr Grantham. 'But, you know, there are private collectors who would be exceedingly excited by such a piece.' He paused. 'Considerable sums of money have been known to change hands. I could make introductions if you are interested?'

Stanley's father reddened. 'Thank you, but I am not at all interested,' he said shortly. 'The place for the thing is in a museum where scientists can study it. What the devil use would it be in the house of some rich gentleman? The world should see it and learn its secrets. How else do we progress? How else do we leave ignorance and superstition behind? You teach geography: you must have some interest in science.'

'Quite so,' said Mr Grantham softly. 'But nobody can study it underground.'

'One day I'll go back.' Stanley could see Henry was stung by the remark. 'One day I'll bring it out. I will!'

'Of course,' soothed Mr Grantham with a smile that Stanley didn't trust. He stubbed out his cigarette. 'You know, we really should be getting back. New term starts in three days – lots to do.'

The train was a monster of green and black iron. Huge clouds of filthy steam billowed from its funnel and from under its wheels as it hauled its coaches through the countryside. Inside, Stanley and his luggage could have been in his own living room. The walls were walnut. The seats were comfortable, and although the carriage rattled a little, he could still eat ice cream out of his Thermos flask without fear of staining his school uniform.

By the time he arrived, most of the other boys were already there. His tardiness didn't bother him: he wasn't new, so had already claimed his place in the dorms. He unpacked quickly and set out to find out what his friends had been up to during the holidays.

Herbert, of course, was already there. His family lived at the school even when it was empty because his father taught there, and he treated the place as his own. Today, he had been asked to make sure all the new boys knew their way around. Instead, he was making sure they knew who was boss.

Once unpacked and signed in, there wasn't much to do until the formal start of school on Monday. The teachers all either had their hands full with the new arrivals, or were preparing their lessons, so Stanley knew he'd be left pretty much to his own devices. He decided to leave the hectic, crowded corridors and take a walk around the grounds.

That was when he spotted the bag. It was a large, thick canvas bag, and it was lying at the back of the school. He noticed it because it was sitting in the middle of a flowerbed, leaning against the wall. It looked as though the bag had been dropped out of the window above, and indeed, the upstairs window above it was still open.

Why would anyone drop a bag out of a window? wondered Stanley.

It was probably someone playing a practical joke. In that case, someone would be in trouble. These were the teachers' living quarters.

He took a closer look. The bag was open at the top, and contained a few old working clothes, a pair of muddy boots, a crowbar and a pickaxe. Underneath them lay some old books and a pile of maps. Stanley was just about to walk away when he noticed something else protruding from the bag. It was a curved metal shape with a rough texture. Stanley recognised it immediately as the handle of a pistol.

'What are you doing there?' The voice came from behind him. He sprang up. Mr Grantham was jogging across the field towards him.

'Nothing, sir,' Stanley replied hastily. 'I just thought...'

'Leave that alone!' snapped Mr Grantham, stopping right in front of him. 'That's mine.' He picked up the bag, obviously flustered. 'It's... erm, quite all right, Stanley. I'm just taking... er... You know you shouldn't be round here. Off you go.' He swung the bag over his shoulder and jogged off towards the school's back gate.

Stanley watched him go. What was that about? Why dump his bag in the flowerbed and then creep round the back of the school to pick it up? If he wanted to go out, why not go out through the front entrance like everyone else? Obviously, he didn't want anyone to know what he was doing.

Stanley waited until his teacher had stepped through the gate before cautiously following him.

At the edge of the field, Stanley flattened himself into the thick hedge that separated the school grounds from the road. He pushed his way through to the inside of the hedge so he couldn't be seen from the road or the school buildings, and edged his way along the fence.

He didn't have to go far before he heard voices.

'You're certain of this?' a gruff voice was saying.

'Yes, it's just sitting there waiting to be dug out. A complete Megalosaurus skull!' Mr Grantham's voice was easily recognisable. 'It'd be the pride of your collection. You'll be the envy of the Royal Society.'

Stanley peered out from between the bushes. The other man was a little older than Mr Grantham and judging by his suit, he was not short of money. On the road beside them, a smart new canvas-sided lorry was parked. It was shiny and black and not at all like the rusty old commercial vehicles Stanley was used to seeing around. Mr Grantham dumped his heavy bag in the open front of the lorry.

'Indeed,' replied the other man. 'Well, if it is there, and it is what you say it is, there'll be plenty in it for you.'

'Thank you, sir,' oozed Mr Grantham. 'There is, of course,' he continued carefully, 'a small question of provenance. Technically, the father of one of my pupils was the first to make the discovery. Technically, the find could be credited to him. Of course, Marchant has some damn fool notion of giving over it to the British Museum.'

'Provenance?' The stranger sniffed. 'My dear boy, its provenance is whatever I say it is.'

Mr Grantham spoke as though he felt obliged to continue. 'Of course, technically, we should seek the permission of the land owner to even search for it.'

'Then we will dig quietly,' said the man. 'Once the find is in the back of my lorry, who's to say where it came from? Plus, if anyone should turn up while we're working, it will be your job to discourage them from asking questions.' He raised an eyebrow at Mr Grantham. 'You are prepared for that eventuality, I suppose?'

'Oh, yes, Mr Hampton,' said Mr Grantham nervously. Stanley thought of the pistol he'd seen nestling in the bottom of the canvas bag. Mr Grantham was prepared all right.

'Then we'd better get going.' Mr Hampton jumped into the driver's seat of the lorry and Mr Grantham got into the other side. The engine coughed into life.

Without stopping to think, Stanley stepped quickly out of the bushes and dived into the back of the lorry. *What am I doing?* he thought to himself, as the vehicle sped off and his school disappeared from sight.

The lorry bumped and rattled along the road. In the back, Stanley held on tight to the leather straps holding the canvas roof in place. The lorry was empty apart from a few sacks and a tarpaulin draped over the metal floor. Stanley already regretted jumping in. He had no idea what was going to happen next or what he could do about it. He had a fair idea of where they were going, but he knew it was a long way from school and he had no way of getting back before he was missed.

As the lorry headed out into the countryside, Stanley tried out a few excuses. Perhaps he had been involved in an accident. Nothing serious, but he'd been knocked unconscious. Maybe he'd seen a robbery and had had to help the police identify suspects. On second thoughts, it might be better to go for something a bit less heroic. Something that didn't sound so much like an adventure. A mundane excuse would be far more convincing. Perhaps he'd just fallen asleep in the library for two days and nobody had noticed.

Suddenly, the lorry turned into a long drive, and pulled up outside a country house. He heard Mr Grantham and Mr Hampton jump out and crunch off across the gravel driveway. Stanley popped his head out of the back of the lorry and looked around. It was a huge house. Newly built, but evidently meant to look like one of the mansions of the rich old families. Mr Hampton had obviously made a lot of money, and recently by the look of it. Most people who'd done that had either played dangerous games on the American stock market, or had somehow turned the war to their advantage.

Stanley heard the crunch of feet on small stones, and saw the two men trudging back across the gravel. Mr Grantham was dragging a wooden box full of heavy mallets, chisels and thick chains and pulleys. Mr Hampton carried equipment more suited to an archaeological dig. He had clearly done this sort of thing before.

Stanley ducked quickly back inside the lorry and looked around. There was nowhere to hide. He only had one chance. He dived under the tarpaulin at the back of the lorry, and lay as still and flat as he could.

He shut his eyes and listened intently as the two men loaded their equipment into the lorry. At any moment they could pull up the tarpaulin or, worse, drop an axe or heavy box on his head. Digging implements clattered onto the floor around him. Then there was silence.

Moments later the engine started. Stanley lifted his head out and sighed with relief.

They didn't stop again for a long time. The lorry's solid tyres did nothing to cushion Stanley from the potholes and bumps in the rough, uneven roadway. As the journey went on, roads made for cars gave way to roads made for horses and carts, and then to winding country lanes made for horses and pedestrians.

Small, ancient villages passed by, the twisting roads taking them first through open farmland, then through wide, flat moorland where ponies, gorse and the odd, incongruous boulder were the only landmarks. Suddenly, the road seemed to close in around them. Dense trees and thick bushes lined the road, making it impossible for Stanley to tell how fast or in what direction they were travelling.

The landscape seemed to confuse the drivers too. Every so often, Stanley was thrown suddenly against the back of the lorry as it lurched to a halt, then backed up, or turned around completely to go back the way it had come. At one point, they stopped completely and Stanley could hear the two men shouting at each other in the front seat. Then the engine started up again and they rattled off in a new direction.

Eventually, they slowed to jogging pace, and turned off the road on to a footpath along the heavily wooded side of a hill. The path turned back and forth as it slowly climbed. Branches scraped along the canvas side of the lorry. For Stanley, it was as though clawed fingers were pushing into the cloth from all sides, trying to grab him.

Now the lorry was moving at walking speed, labouring over every bump and pothole in the path. It lurched and rocked so much, Stanley thought it might topple over, but they kept going, back and forth and upward.

Eventually, the path came to an end and the lorry turned off into the woods. The engine revved hard as the lorry struggled over the crest of the hill, then tipped forward alarmingly as they bounced downhill over thick brambles, lurching and shuddering as they negotiated their way around trees and over boulders.

When the driver finally gave up and cut the engine, they were perched at a precarious angle against a tree stump. Stanley heard the front doors open and looked quickly around the sparse interior of the lorry.

They would surely find him now. There was nowhere to hide, and in any case they'd obviously reached their destination so they'd be unloading the equipment any second.

He waited, frozen to the spot, but nobody came. Cautiously, he crept to the back of the lorry and peered out. There was still no sign of the two men. He hopped out of the back and ducked into the woods, then made his way around to the front. *They don't want to unload their tools until they've found what they're looking for,* he thought.

He felt around at the front of the lorry and flipped open the bonnet. Underneath was a complex array of gears, levers and moulded metal. Behind the main engine block, a nest of cables connected the engine to the cab. He wrapped his shirt cuff around his hand to protect himself from the hot engine, grabbed the wires and yanked. Two or three of them gave way immediately. Another tug released the rest. *That should slow them down a little,* thought Stanley, as he quietly closed the bonnet.

He crept deeper into the woods, striking out in front of the lorry – he knew they must have gone that way otherwise he'd have seen or heard them. The trees were old and thick, and where their branches allowed light down to the ground, wild tangles of brambles grew.

It didn't take long to find the two men. They were talking loudly and scanning the woods ahead as they walked. Stanley followed quietly.

Suddenly, Mr Grantham shouted, 'There it is!' and ran off.

Mr Hampton followed, slightly less nimbly. Stanley heard him say, 'By Jove, that could well be it!'

He dodged forward and hid behind the double trunk of a large tree. As he looked out, he recognised what appeared to be the tomb from his father's sketch. The mossy stones, the worn carvings around the stone door, everything was as his father had drawn it.

Squinting, Stanley could just make out some of the animals depicted in the carvings. Some he recognised. Others seemed to be strange, mythical beasts. There were unicorns, snakes with wings, even dragons.

'Well, what are you waiting for?' snapped Mr Hampton.

Mr Grantham stepped forward and tried pushing the huge stone door inwards. It didn't budge. He wriggled his fingers into the crack between the doorway and the stone and pulled hard. The stone rocked a little, yet remained unmoved.

'Come on!' Mr Grantham said, looking back at Mr Hampton. 'If we both pull...'

The other man didn't need any encouragement. He found enough of a gap along the top of the door for his chubby fingers, and pushed them in. Mr Grantham did the same on the other side of the stone and they pulled together. The stone rocked again.

Encouraged, they yanked even harder this time, and the stone slowly started to tip. As it overbalanced, they both stepped back out of its way, but it only dropped a few feet before it was blocked by a tree-trunk.

'Can you get through?' Mr Hampton asked. Mr Grantham climbed on to the rock and tried to lower himself in to the tomb. He managed to get one leg through the door, but no matter how he positioned himself, he couldn't fit his body through the narrow gap. Frustrated, he finally gave up. 'We'll have to smash our way in,' he huffed, brushing the dirt from his trousers. 'Come on, let's get the picks.'

The men headed back to the lorry, leaving Stanley alone.

Although the gap in the doorway was too small for a grown man, it was just big enough for Stanley. He knew he was taking a huge risk, as Mr Hampton and Mr Grantham could be back at any moment. But he had to go in. The skull from his father's drawing had been watching him for his entire life. There was no way he could leave now without looking it in the eye.

He hauled himself up to the top of the rock door and slid down into the darkness.

CHAPTER 9

STANLEY MARCHANT: 1932

At first they were just shapes in the rock. Nothing made sense in the darkness. Just rough patches and smooth patches on the surface of the wall. Slowly, though, Stanley's eyes adjusted and the tomb began to reveal its host.

Ridges of light reflecting from the doorway traced strange angles. Here, a long, curved tooth. There, an oval loop flowing from the rock. Underneath, a long, straight line with tiny pockmarks all the way along, sloping diagonally back and down towards the floor.

Suddenly, he realised he was tracing the line of the inside of the creature's jaw. Teeth jutted out above it. Towards the throat, they were small, the size of Stanley's fingers. As he followed them up the wall, they became larger, thicker, and began to curve inwards, down towards the throat. He brushed heavy, dusty cobwebs from the wall, and began to see details on the teeth, serrations for cutting and tearing at meat.

When this creature lived, Stanley thought, *nothing that saw those teeth close up would have had a chance.* The thought made him step back, and suddenly he could see it all. The whole shape of the skull, embedded in the rock in front of him.

It was just as he had imagined it from his father's painting. There was the huge eye, the solid jaw. It gave off the same feeling as the painting, a mixture of fear and a magnetic attraction that made you feel as if you could never look away. Part of him wanted to turn, run up the steps and climb out over the stone door. But he did not. Instead, he felt his hand rising towards the wall. Gently, he pushed through layers of cobwebs weighed down with grit and dead spiders, to touch the fossilised snout. The stone felt smooth and cold.

In Stanley's mind, he could feel the creature breathing.

Suddenly, a sharp, hard chiming snapped Stanley's attention away from the wall. He looked around, confused. The sound came again, a loud, ringing impact, disappearing into the darkness.

He realised with horror that it was the sound of a pickaxe striking stone.

It rang out again, and then again almost immediately. Mr Hampton and Mr Grantham were back. Now Stanley could hear them shouting to each other as they hacked away at the stone.

Panicking, Stanley looked around. The tomb was a single, tiny room. It had just one exit, and aside from the gaping head of its fossilised resident, it was completely empty. The moment the two men broke through the doorway, he would be seen and caught. There was no way out this time.

His mind racing, he searched the floor. No hidden trapdoors. He looked up at the ceiling. Nothing. He felt his way to the back of the tomb. The wall dipped in a little at the corner, but there was no crevice big enough to hide in. Outside, he could hear the rock beginning to splinter and crack. Encouraged, the two men were swinging their pickaxes at it harder and faster.

Stanley only had one chance, and he would have to get it exactly right. He crept up the stone stairs towards the doorway. The rock was vibrating as it was struck again and again, and small pieces of dirt and dust were raining down from the top of it. Through the gap in the doorway, Stanley could see the effort in the men's faces as they hacked away. The inside of the tomb was dark, and the men could not see him as he squinted out, but the moment the slab broke, he would be standing right in front of them.

If he timed this wrong, he could easily be injured by a pickaxe, or worse.

The sound of picks against stone was painful to his ears now, and underneath it he could hear the stone cracking more and more with each blow.

He hooked his fingers around the doorframe, leaned back into the tomb and waited, holding his breath.

Suddenly, a sound like a gunshot burst through the air. The stone slab split across the middle from one side to the other, the two halves folding outwards. The bottom half crashed down onto the top step, the upper half toppling onto it.

As the two men stepped back to avoid being hit by the slab, Stanley took his chance. He leapt up on top of the stone as it fell, hauling himself forward, and bounded out of the door.

His way may have been blocked, but the one thing the two men were not expecting was for a living body to come flying out of the tomb in a cloud of dust.

Mr Grantham was the smaller of the two men, so Stanley ran straight at him. He hit him low and hard, barging the startled teacher out of the way and sprinting off into the forest.

A second later, Stanley heard Mr Hampton shout after him as the two men gave chase. Then there was a loud bang. This one really was a gunshot. They were shooting at him! He dodged between the trees and threw himself downhill, sweeping branches out of his face as he struggled to keep upright.

Stanley was a fast runner, but the sounds of the men behind him didn't seem to get any quieter as he ploughed onwards. He glanced back and could see them pelting after him. Mr Grantham was clutching the gun and running hard, but luckily he couldn't get a clear shot through the trees. Mr Hampton was much slower. Even so, Stanley could see him circling around to try and cut off his escape route further downhill.

Panicking, Stanley looped around and started struggling uphill, away from Mr Hampton. At the same time, Mr Grantham began to catch up with him, his long strides making short work of the rough terrain. At the brow of the hill the trees thinned out, which Stanley knew would make him an easy target. Keeping as low as possible, he zigzagged back and forth between bramble thickets, hoping and praying that he could avoid giving his teacher a clear aim. A shot cracked through the air. Stanley tensed, but felt nothing. Mr Grantham had missed. Diving over the brow of the hill, Stanley hurtled downwards, grabbing the trunks of trees as he fell past them, desperately trying to stay on his feet. Another shot echoed past him, but this time it was a wild attempt and splintered off a tree some way ahead.

A couple of seconds later, Stanley's feet found a level, flat path. He turned onto it and sprinted as fast as he could. The track wound back and forth down the side of the hill. Although he could run faster here, the clear, open way would give Mr Grantham more of a chance to shoot.

Stanley glanced back. His teacher was nowhere to be seen as the path doubled back on itself, working its way down the hill.

Stanley thought fast. *Mr Grantham has obviously seen me take the path,* he reasoned, *and has headed straight down the hill to cut me off. I need to watch out.*

Up ahead, the road snaked down and around again, but Stanley couldn't see what was around the corner because the trees were too thick. *That's an ideal spot for an ambush*, he decided. Instead of turning the corner, he ploughed off the path and into the trees. Turning sharply downhill, he ran on.

Behind him, he heard Mr Grantham curse and crash into the forest after him.

Stanley's lungs were burning. He wouldn't be able to keep up this pace for long. Luckily, the ground was beginning to level out, and up ahead he could see the edge of the woods. Beyond the tree line he could even see houses. He clenched his fists for one final burst of speed and forced his legs to keep moving.

Minutes later, he crashed out of the wood and into an open field. If he could just reach the house on the other side... Another gunshot rang out from close behind him as he dodged and swerved erratically, trying to present the most difficult target possible to his attacker. The gun fired again as Stanley, miraculously uninjured, leapt over the back gate of the house and pounded on its door.

The old man who opened the door looked kindly enough. 'Can I help you?' he enquired.

Stanley realised he must look quite a state. 'I wonder if you'd mind letting me in?' he said as politely as he could manage. 'My geography teacher is trying to kill me.'

Mr Grantham and Mr Hampton realised the game was up as soon as Stanley made it to the house. They hovered around outside for a couple of minutes, then disappeared back into the trees. Meanwhile, the old gentleman called the police. The pair were still standing over the lorry arguing about how to fix it when they were arrested.

After a cup of sweet tea Stanley telephoned his father, who listened in worried silence while he recounted everything that had happened. When he finished, he expected anger. Instead, his father simply sighed in relief.

'Stay there,' he said. 'I'll come immediately.'

Stanley thought about how his father had spoken of the village he grew up in, and how he'd reacted when anyone suggested returning there. 'You don't have to come,' he said. 'Really, I'm quite all right, and I'm sure the police can take me back to school.'

'I'll come,' said his father with determination. 'Can I speak with the gentleman who rescued you?'

Stanley handed the phone to the old gentleman. He heard his father thank the man.

'Not at all, not at all,' the old man said. 'You have a well-brought-up young lad there. And an uncommonly brave one.'

Stanley's father asked for directions to the house. The old man replied, 'No need. If you can find your way into the village just ask anyone. Everyone here knows me. You see, I'm the vicar here.'

There was a long pause, and the line went dead.

Two hours later, there was a knock at the door. The old man opened it, with Stanley at his side. Stanley's father stood in the doorway. He said nothing, but there was an odd look in his eyes. Stanley almost thought he might have been about to cry. He stared at the old man for a long time.

At last he spoke. 'Stanley,' he said, without looking at his son, 'I'd like you to meet your grandfather.'

Excavated, cleaned and mounted on wires, the skull was an impressive sight. Each bone had been painstakingly prepared. The rock around it had been chipped and polished away one tiny piece at a time with chisels and needles designed for dentists and tapestry makers. Once complete, the skull had been reassembled with every tooth replaced in its socket and every crack invisibly sealed.

Stanley had watched as it was brought out from the ground by a team led by his father, and he had visited the workshop often during the preparation work. Now, Stanley and Henry sat together on stage as the lecture theatre filled with scientists and academics. The skull sat at the centre of the stage looking out into the audience. Dramatic lights were arranged around it, although it needed no such theatre. The creature had such presence that everyone who looked at it froze for a second, as though turned to stone, before settling into their seats.

He fingered his typewritten speech and looked at his father who smiled reassuringly. The audience was intimidating, but they were both clear on what they were going to say. Stanley would tell the story of the skull's discovery, and his father would follow it up with a detailed description of the megalosaurus itself, outlining how it fitted into an evolutionary tree that connected it to the American tyrannosaurus and allosaurus, and more distantly to mammals, apes and humans. The audience quietened, a short introduction was made, and father and son stood up to present their find to the scientific community.

As they started to speak, nobody noticed the old vicar slip in to the back of the auditorium, quietly take a seat, and begin to listen.

CHAPTER 10

CARL MARCHANT: 2014

A zombie. That was it. Carl Marchant had been trying to work out what living at home was like these days, and he'd finally got it. It was like living with a zombie. As Mum leant against the breakfast table, her head flopped from side to side as though her neck wasn't strong enough to hold it upright. Her eyes were red and sunk back in her skull. Her skin looked grey, and her hair stuck out on one side and fell limply across her face on the other.

Tiredness was half of it. She had to do everything herself now, and after two months the strain of pretending things were just fine had begun to tell.

Things were not fine. In fact, they were far from it. And it was time for Carl to deal with the other half of the problem. It was time to take on the dinosaur and bring Dad back.

He swiped the screen of his phone and tapped it to bring up the bus route. It was an easy enough journey, although he'd never made it alone before. He looked up. Mum was staring into the distance with a living-dead blankness in her eyes.

'I'm going to the park with Gerry after school,' he said, as casually as he could. He watched for her response, hoping she didn't ask too many questions.

'Mmm...' Mum grunted. 'What?'

'Is that OK?'

'Um... yes. Yes, fine.' She hadn't even listened to what he'd said. Carl thought this was how teenagers were supposed to behave, not parents. He grabbed his bag and left, holding a piece of toast.

The school day seemed long, and Carl spent most of it thinking about Mum and Dad. The teachers had started smiling randomly at him, so obviously they all knew. Mum's behaviour was difficult, but completely understandable. She was trying to hold everything together, but it wasn't working. It was as simple as that.

As for Dad... This time, it was too much.

Dad had always been a bit flaky, albeit in a precise sort of way. He could be distant sometimes, drifting off into his own little world, or getting caught up in things that didn't seem to matter to anyone else. Other adults tended to get a bit fidgety around him if he talked to them for too long, but that was because they didn't really get him.

There was another side to Dad, which most people never saw. If you got him interested in what you were doing, then he was right there with you. He would follow it, whatever it was, to its natural, fantastic, impossible conclusion, and be as excited by it and into it as you were.

Carl remembered reading a story once with Dad about people living on Mars, and wondering why nobody had built a base there. Pretty soon, they'd started talking about how far away it was and how difficult it would be to make a self-supporting base that didn't need constant supplies of food and oxygen from Earth.

Within a couple of weeks, they'd taken a big bottle of water and worked out what kind of bacteria they'd need. They'd ordered them through the lab and put in some plants to create oxygen. Finally, they'd added their colonists – a pair of freshwater shrimps – and sealed up the bottle.

Everything in the bottle was designed to create a self-sustaining ecosystem. The plants created oxygen, the shrimp ate the plants, and the bacteria recycled the waste. All it needed was sunlight.

Now, a year later, the bottle still sat on Carl's windowsill. The two shrimp astronauts were still thriving. In fact, Carl had noticed, they'd just laid tiny eggs that stuck to the plants' leaves. He wanted to tell Dad. But Dad was gone.

When the bell rang, Carl was on his feet and out of the school gates in under a minute. He got to the bus stop just in time, took the short ride to the station and reached the platform just as a tube was pulling in.

From the Underground, it was a short jog to the museum. The place was like a cathedral, grand and imposing, but instead of carvings of saints and crosses, the exterior alcoves were carved with the images of animals, living and extinct, in soft, rounded stone. Carl walked up the wide stone steps and under the arch. The head of the diplodocus skeleton in the main hall hung in the air above his head, impossibly small compared to its enormous body.

He ignored it, walking through the main hall and along one of the side galleries to a small door with a combination lock. He'd been here often enough with Dad and he couldn't be expected to look away every time someone entered a security code. He keyed in the number and stepped through.

The offices of the museum were a stark contrast to the cavernous galleries. They were a maze of corridors, tiny labs, offices and storerooms. Most of the museum's enormous collection was not on display, but was stored in rows and rows of huge, grey cabinets. Carl's dad had told him that there were so many fossils here that many weren't even catalogued or named.

He walked on past them, deeper into the warren of corridors until he came to a grey door. He quietly pushed it open and stepped inside.

The room was part office, part lab. At the front sat a desk with an open laptop on it. Ordinarily, anyone sitting at the desk would have been able to look directly out of the window and down over London. Right now, however, their view would be obscured by a huge skull with curved, serrated teeth. Whoever sat at the desk now would be met, each time they glanced up from their work, by the gaping jaws of a megalosaurus, poised as if about to strike, empty eye sockets glaring straight down at them.

Along one wall was an arrangement of lab equipment, some bottles of liquid and a centrifuge. Next to it sat a large, powerful microscope and a figure in a crumpled blue suit, completely oblivious to Carl's presence.

'Hello, Dad,' said Carl. Dad looked up. He was grey and drawn. He looked as though he hadn't eaten for a week. Carl sighed. The living dead again. Dad managed a smile. It looked real, but forced at the same time. As though the intention to smile was there, but the muscles needed to produce one were out of condition.

'Hello.'

'I just thought I'd come to see you...' Carl wasn't really sure what to say.

'Yes?' Dad replied. There was a long pause.

To break the silence, Carl said, 'So this is the skull?'

Dad brightened noticeably and seized on the chance to talk about something easy. 'Beautiful, isn't she? I say *she* just because of the size, of course. Can't be sure.' He looked up at the skull. 'Look at the way the eyes face forwards – typical predator, you see, so she can judge distance when she's hunting.' He started to describe the teeth and the muscles that attached the jaw, even going so far as to explain how the creature's brain would have been arranged within the skull.

Carl interrupted him. 'Mum wants you to come back home,' he said. 'We both do.'

'Of course,' Dad continued, ignoring Carl's interjection, 'what I'm interested in is inside the bones.' He dragged his eyes away from the skull and walked back to the microscope.

'I know you get caught up in your work,' Carl pressed on, 'but this – this is more than that. This is serious now. You can see that, can't you?'

Dad had got wrapped up in work before. Sometimes he'd been distant and hard to reach, but there had always been a way to get through to him. To bring him back. This time was different. He'd never let it go this far before. He'd never moved out before.

'You see,' his father continued, a far-off look on his face, 'what I've done is taken a shaving of bone, and used a fairly standard sort of test but with a bit of a twist, and – '

'A test for what?' snapped Carl, caving in to his father's obsession.

'DNA.'

'Dinosaur DNA?' Carl looked incredulous.

Everyone knew fossils were just stone. There was no DNA in stone.

'Take a look at this.' Dad gestured to the microscope. 'She's more alive than you think!'

In spite of himself, Carl moved over to the microscope and peered into it. Blurry yellow shapes drifted in front of the lens. They shifted and changed as he scanned the slide and changed the focus the way Dad had taught him. Carl had seen DNA through a microscope before. In fact, they'd extracted it at home using strawberries, a bottle of vodka and some washing-up liquid. He'd seen its long, ghostly strands scattered over the slides they'd prepared together, and if there was one thing he was certain of, it was that what he was looking at here wasn't DNA.

He stood away from the eyepiece. 'I can't see anything,' he said. 'It's just bits of stone.'

Dad grabbed the eyepiece and stooped to stare down into it. He clenched his teeth in disappointment. 'It was there!' He scanned the slide quickly from one side to the other. 'You've lost it!'

No, thought Carl. *You're the one who's lost it*.

Instead he said, 'I'll come back later, shall I?' Dad just waved him away without looking up from the slide.

Chapter 11

Carl Marchant: 2014

Mum had been crying, that much was obvious, but she'd also been doing something else. Something much worse. She had been packing.

Flat-packed boxes were piled around the living room. Some were empty, some were full. There was no order that Carl could see to the work. It was as though she had simply started to throw everything they owned into crates.

When Carl had arrived home, he'd found her sat in the middle of the floor. She had been caught, midway through her work, by a photo album that she'd made the mistake of opening. Her expression, as she slowly turned the pages, said everything and nothing at the same time.

She looked up at him as he walked in. 'Grandma and Grandad have offered to put us up for a while. After that, we can find somewhere up near them.' There was a resigned tone to her voice.

'Dad will come back!' Carl tried to sound more confident than he felt. 'You know how he is... he just needs to work it out. He just needs time.'

'I've given him time. So much time,' she said quietly. 'I can't do it any more.' She closed the photo album and put it in the box next to her.

'I don't want to leave school,' Carl lied. 'I'm settled there.'

Uprooting Carl from school had always been the strongest argument Mum or Dad could ever come up with for not moving. Every time either of them had thought about the possibility of moving to a less expensive area, or a city with better job prospects, the subject of Carl's schooling had come up and that had put an end to it. Carl, apparently, was 'settled' where he was, and that was that.

In truth, Carl wasn't bothered. School was OK. He could take it or leave it. He had friends there, and he had enemies, just as he would anywhere else. Starting a new school might actually be quite fun, and anyway, there'd always be Facebook.

But Carl wasn't ready to give up. Dad had gone deep this time, deeper than he'd ever been. In his mind, he was lost in a Jurassic jungle, but Carl was sure there was a way back. There was always a way back.

He just needed time to work on him. There was no sense trying to force him back to reality – that risked driving him deeper still. You simply had to be there and wait for him to come around.

'How long have we got?' he asked.

'I've already spoken to your school,' she said. 'We're moving on Saturday'.

'The day after tomorrow?' Carl felt as if he'd been hit in the stomach. He only had one day?

'I'm sorry. I really am, but if I don't do it now...' She trailed off. 'You're going to have to say goodbye to your friends at school tomorrow.'

The next day however, Carl did not say goodbye to his friends, because he didn't go to school. Instead, he got straight on the underground to the museum. There was no time to wait for Dad to come around now. It was now or never.

He punched in the entry code and walked purposefully up to the grey door to the lab. Then he paused. He realised he had no plan. Slowly he turned the handle and pushed.

Dad was sitting at his desk, his back to the door. He had his elbows on the table and his hands up to his face. He was staring up at the huge skeletal face hanging above him, looking into its empty, glaring eyes.

'Where are you sleeping?' Carl said quietly. Dad turned. He looked as though he wasn't sleeping anywhere, but he nodded towards the corner of the room. A sleeping bag was rolled up against the wall. He looked back at his laptop screen. It was covered in a pattern of red, blue and green blocks arranged in a complex grid.

'It's human,' he said dejectedly.

'What's human?'

'The DNA on the slide. It's human.'

'You have to snap out of this right now, Dad,' said Carl.

Dad's eyes suddenly widened, as though an idea had struck him. 'Did you touch the slide?' he demanded accusingly.

'What?'

'It was contaminated with human DNA,' he snapped. 'And it's not mine!'

'I didn't touch it,' sighed Carl.

'What about the skull? Did you touch the skull?'

'No, Dad, I didn't. It could have come from anywhere!' Carl almost yelled.

'But you were here. You were *in* here.' Dad looked angry. Angry and desperate. He was standing now, pointing at Carl. 'You could have accidentally – '

'Mum wants to move.' Carl cut him off. 'Tomorrow.'

Dad stopped for a second, frozen as though part of him had suddenly glimpsed what was really happening to his life. Then the other part kicked in. 'This is a laboratory!' he barked. 'It's not a place for children!' Behind his shoulder, the skull watched them with predatory eyes.

'Did you hear me?' Carl said each word, slowly and deliberately. 'We... are... moving... tomorrow.'

Again, Dad paused. Carl knew he was on very dangerous ground. 'Look, I'm sorry,' he said quietly. 'I'm sorry there was no DNA. But that's it now. You know there's nothing there. It's over. You can come back.'

Dad looked at Carl, then back at the skull.

'It's only a fossil, Dad. Is it really worth losing everything for a piece of rock?' Carl searched his father's eyes for some kind of recognition. And there *was* something there. Carl saw his eyes dart one way and another, as though he was a hunted animal looking for a way out. He was thinking, beginning to understand...

Suddenly, he gasped, 'No! No. That was just one sample.' He stepped towards Carl, grabbing his shoulders, smiling a triumphant smile. Carl's heart sank. 'I've got dozens of samples. They're all scanned. They're all on the hard drive.' He pointed at the laptop on the table in front of the skull. 'I will find it!'

That was it. Carl had lost him. There was no way back now. No hope. That computer held enough work to keep Dad obsessed for months. More than long enough to destroy him, and his family. Carl looked into his father's eyes. They were filled with a strange and desperate energy.

Carl wrenched himself free from Dad's grip and grabbed a flask of liquid from the bench next to the microscope. The liquid was clear and the flask unlabelled, but Carl knew what it was. It was strong acid for dissolving stone. He yanked out the stopper, and before Dad could stop him, he poured the contents over the laptop keyboard.

The screen went blank instantly and there was a fizzing, buzzing sound as the liquid soaked through the keys and started to burn through the hard drive. Fumes began to rise in front of the skull's snout.

Dad was staring at the laptop in horror, his mouth hanging open. 'What have you done?' he screamed, rushing towards the corroded computer.

Carl barged into his father, blocking his way. From behind him he felt a heat on his back like the breath of a dinosaur. Dad pulled back one arm, clenching his fist. Carl closed his eyes.

Nothing happened.

He slowly opened his eyes again. Dad was standing in front of him, head and shoulders down. He was shaking.

'I... I'm sorry,' he started. 'I'm so, so sorry.'

Carl paused. 'I've ruined your laptop,' he said.

Dad shook his head. His eyes were full of tears. 'It's OK. There was nothing important on it anyway.' He reached out his arms and held Carl for a long time.

'Come on,' he said eventually. 'It's time to go home.'

At the door, Dad stopped and looked back at the skull, still staring down at them. 'My grandfather discovered it, you know,' he said.

'I know.'

'I just wanted to add something to it. You understand?'

Carl shrugged. 'Sort of,' he said.

'I hope your mother will take me back,' Dad said finally, after another long pause. 'I've been an idiot.'

I hope so too, thought Carl.

CHAPTER 12
JOHN MARCHANT: 2201

People were always asking John Marchant what it was like to be the first Martian. He never really knew how to answer them. The truth was, it wasn't like anything. It was just his life. He was born here on the base. It was as simple as that. He didn't know what it was like *not* to be the first Martian.

He made a pointing gesture inside the mechanised suit and it reacted instantly, uncurling one long metal finger. He made a tapping movement and the finger's chisel-like end stabbed at a piece of rock, splitting it neatly along its seam so that it opened up like a billion-year-old book.

He examined the inside of the rock. It was smooth, featureless. Just another blank page in Mars' history.

He tossed the rock away. It bounced high in the low gravity and toppled down the side of the crater, sending up flurries of dust.

He looked over his shoulder at his parents, who were digging a little further down the slope. None of them had been able to resist one last dig before they left, probably forever. John turned back to look at the base.

When he was very small, the base consisted of six domes growing just enough food to feed him, his parents and a couple of other scientists. They had needed constant supplies from Earth, which roared in on shuttles every couple of months, bringing strange surprises like toys and chocolate. It had always seemed to John that Earth was a far more interesting place than Mars and yet, oddly, everyone he got emails from seemed fascinated by their cramped little home.

Slowly, the base had grown. Day and night the automated foundry churned out iron and clay bricks of different sizes, and everything from buildings to toothbrush handles were built from them. The blocks were solid, interchangeable and on Mars, they were light enough to build almost anything with. They were the secret of the base's success, and meant that the old glass-roofed domes were being slowly crowded out by windowless and mostly empty cube-shaped buildings.

They were self-sufficient in most things now. Food, fuel – there was even a pod for growing synthesised meat, although John was constantly told that it didn't taste like the real thing. What held up the base nowadays wasn't a lack of space or food. It was electronics. That was why many of the new buildings stood empty. The base just didn't have the processing power available to manage their temperatures and work their doors.

Nowadays, the traffic from Earth had slowed and most of the transports were in the opposite direction, Mars exporting materials rather than importing them. So no more chocolate. And tomorrow, they would export John and his parents.

He looked back at his dad, hacking out and smashing one rock after another before tossing it into the crater, and his mother picking slowly and deliberately through every stone in front of her. He knew neither of them would leave if it were up to them. This was *his* decision, and they'd agreed for the sake of his future.

John lifted another small slab of rock and split it. Nothing unusual. He threw it away. There never was anything. Or at least there never was *the* thing. Every day since he could remember, his parents or the other scientists on the base had gone out to the crater, and chipped away at the ground there. Even today, on their last day on Mars, they couldn't resist the urge to go back out.

Over fifteen years, his parents had excavated the rocks that told the history of the planet in layers. Every day they had learned more about that history and returned with more samples to analyse in the labs. They rarely even spoke about what they were really hoping for.

Every few years, someone would find something. A microscopic pattern embedded in the rock that could have been a fossil. A different kind of rock that might have once been organic. But each time it had been examined, it had come to nothing. There were no fossils on Mars. At least, no undisputed ones. Except the old megalosaurus in the centre dome. The skull was always present, glowering down from a plinth to remind them why they were there.

John stepped back and looked at the side of the crater, which swept out in a huge wide curve. Whatever had hit the ground here had carved a great scoop out of the side of the planet, and around its edge layers of rock, each a subtly different colour from those above, were exposed. The further down the crater you went, the further back in time you could explore.

The base concentrated its effort on a few layers of rock from a time when oceans had flowed here. Thick bands of dark red-brown ran around the edge of the crater, broken by landslides and cliffs.

As John stood back, he could suddenly see that the layer he'd been working on was actually two similar coloured bands separated by a third thin layer of pale rock in the middle.

Why hasn't anyone spotted this before? he wondered. He followed the broken, pencil-thin line. It was faint, but he could see it. Another type of sediment, different to what was above and below it. A few million years of unexplored time.

He grasped a loose rock from the pale band, edged it out of the crater wall and tapped it lightly. As it fell easily into two flat plates, John stared at it, unable to believe what he was seeing.

On the inside edge of one of the pieces, a long, snaking line made its way in loops through the rock. It looked like a tiny trail tunnelled into soft mud before the rock set hard.

'Dad...' he whispered. Then he shouted, 'Mum, Dad, over here!' His parents looked up, and lumbered over in their clumsy suits.

'I've never seen anything like it,' Dad's radio hissed in his ear, 'at least not *here*.'

'Is it – ' started John.

Dad interrupted him. 'It's not a good idea to start guessing about what it is and what it isn't,' he said, but his eyes were huge. 'We'll take it home. There'll be some people with opinions there, no doubt.'

It was funny how Dad always called Earth 'home', despite not having lived there for fifteen years. As he looked down at the stone with its mysterious looping tunnel, it occurred to John that he was probably the only person who didn't call Earth home, and that was probably what it was like being the first Martian.

John pushed hard with both legs and levered the iron weight into the air. He held it for a count of five, let it fall back, and pushed again, just as he'd been taught. This exercise was hard work, but it got him away from everyone else, and that was where he wanted to be right now. Too much going round in his head.

Besides, with a journey of six months in an enforced coma ahead of him, his muscles would have to be in top shape for him to have a chance of even being able to stand when he got to Earth. And John was absolutely determined that when the hatch opened, he would walk out of it, not be ferried out on a stretcher as everyone assumed he'd be.

John was well aware that on Earth he was quite a celebrity. And there was no way he was going to disappoint his fans. First impressions were important. And when you were starting a new school on an alien planet, he imagined they were vital. He clenched his teeth and pushed his legs out. The iron weight creaked upwards. He counted slowly to five, watched by the skull's great, empty eye, and then relaxed.

To John, the skull was the only object in the base that seemed genuinely natural. Its huge eye sockets were sculpted into complex but perfect curves. Its teeth were detailed with tiny serrations, every tooth different from every other. Each part of the skull had its own purpose, unique and yet fitting exactly with every other part, built and shaped by an impossibly intricate and brutal form of evolution. The skull, unlike anything else around him, could never have been invented. There were no standard-sized bricks here.

It sat in the centre of the dome, raised on an iron plinth. Its presence was symbolic: it was a mascot, a trademark and a connection to the Earth and its history. It felt to John as out of place on Mars as he would be on Earth. It was such an impossible, impractical object to ship to Mars. John thought that was probably why Dad had done it.

As he stared up into its enormous jaws, he was suddenly struck by how fragile it was. How alone.

That was when he heard the sound. It was a noise like cracking ice and he knew instantly what it was. It was the sound that everyone on the base feared and to which everyone was trained to react. The outer dome was breaking.

The hardened glass was arranged as a tough network of hexagonal pieces, but occasionally a rock whipped up by the fierce Mars winds could break one of the pieces and cause the dome to de-pressurise.

John looked up. One hexagonal piece was marked with a thin line, and the fracture was splitting out across the surface in a widening star. Instantly, sensors detected the danger and there was a metallic clang as all doors into the rest of the complex were locked down.

John was trapped.

Any second, the glass would shatter and all the air, followed by everything that wasn't fixed to the ground, would be sucked out through the hexagonal hole. He frantically looked around.

He had one chance. He leapt towards the outside door. His suit stood where he'd left it, like a robotic sentry. He could hear the crack in the glass widening as he hauled himself inside and started to fasten the catches around his legs and arms.

The cracking sound turned into the roar of escaping air. John felt himself being pulled upwards. The suit was magnetised and anchored itself to the floor, but only one of the catches was fully fastened around his leg and he could feel himself being wrenched upwards and out of the suit. Using all his strength, he dragged his arms down and grabbed the other catch, forcing it closed.

As he hauled first one arm, then the other into the suit, plants were being uprooted all around him and were flying up towards the ceiling. His exercise machine was shaking from side to side, the weights detaching themselves one by one and hurling themselves upwards.

As he fought with the final catch which would seal the suit around his head, John could feel the air being sucked out of his lungs. Everything in the room was spinning around him, and the blood rushing around his skull made his head swim. Fighting against blacking out, he finally managed to close the last catch.

The sound from outside was cut off, and there was a gentle hiss as air was fed into the bubble around his head.

Outside, the dome was a silent vortex of swirling plants and iron and ceramic blocks. Everything spun around and upwards, like a bath emptying through a plughole.

John fought to calm his breath, and as he looked into the centre of the vortex, he suddenly saw the skull. It was moving. The creature's head was rocking back and forth on its mountings. The great eyes stared straight at him, but the jaw was tipping back, gaping wider and wider as the rushing air tore at it.

It was stone, but it was brittle. If it came loose, it would be smashed to pieces. John looked across the dome. Where he stood, he was safe, shielded by the outside doorway. If he stepped into the centre of the room, his suit could be hit by any of the flying debris, dislodged from the floor, or punctured. But if he didn't move, the skull would be destroyed.

Somehow, he couldn't be its executioner.

He stepped forward into the vortex. An iron table flew at his head and he ducked. It bounced into the side of the dome and rolled upwards. He took another step and almost lost his footing in the clumsy suit.

Centimetre by centimetre he edged forward. The skull was rocking alarmingly now. Three of the four bolts holding it down had rattled free, and it was pitching loosely from side to side. John could see the final bolt beginning to tear from its mounting.

Suddenly, it gave way. The skull toppled forward, its gaping mouth lurching toward him. He took a huge step forward and raised both hands, grabbing the jaw and the top of the eye socket. The suit's motors ground, adding just enough to his own strength to hold the stone structure steady.

He locked the hands of the suit in place and held on while the vortex around him slowly calmed. He was still in the same position when his parents and the rest of the crew finally sealed the dome and rescued him.

When the shuttle was loaded for the journey back to Earth, it had an extra passenger. The beds in which

John and his parents were due to spend the voyage had to be hastily re-positioned further from the cargo doors, and the shuttle's computer was instructed to re-calculate its weight, speed and fuel estimates to take into account the additional mass of a fossilised megalosaurus skull. With the leisure dome damaged, the museum that had loaned the skull to the Martian base quickly came to the conclusion that they wanted it safely back on Earth.

John was the first to be fitted into his cocoon-like bed for launch. Mum and Dad were standing over him, checking the various instruments and making sure everything was perfect for the journey. It was supposed to be a relaxing experience, and the computer was piping soft music through the ship. However, instead of enjoying the gently reassuring atmosphere, the three of them were having a massive row.

'Just don't ever do anything like that ever again!' yelled Mum. She wasn't at all happy that he'd taken the risk of trying to save the skull.

'When am I going to have the opportunity to do it again?' protested John.

'He's got a point,' chuckled Dad, trying to defuse the situation.

'You know exactly what I'm talking about,' snapped Mum, 'and he only did it because of you!'

'Why because of me?' cried Dad. He turned back to John. 'Your mother's right, you know. We just want you to be safe. It was very irresponsible.'

Mum was still glaring at Dad. 'He knows how much that fossil means to you!' she shouted.

Dad shrugged in frustration.

John tried to sit up. 'I can make my own decisions, you know. I'm better at driving a suit than you give me credit for,' he started, as Mum pushed him back down into the bed.

'We have to get you fixed for the flight,' she said dismissively. 'Hold still.'

Mum and Dad did the rest of the pre-flight checks in silence, then said a short, 'Goodnight,' to John before going to their own beds and strapping themselves in. John looked up at the ceiling. It was a shiny metal angled plate that reflected the far end of the cargo bay. The skull, the last item to board the ship, was being winched into place. It stared back at him as though the creature was standing over his bed.

'How long is the journey exactly?' he whispered to the ship's computer.

Its voice was neutral. 'I don't know,' it said. 'A better question would be: "how long is the journey approximately?"'

John sighed. 'OK. How long is the journey *approximately*?'

'Four thousand, five hundred and forty hours,' it said. 'We could travel faster, but that would cause unnecessary risks.'

'What kind of risks?'

'A new wormhole accelerator is running just outside of the Earth's orbit. We must avoid crossing its acceleration vectors at critical points during the preliminary experimental phases.'

'What?' said John, feeling confused. 'Why?'

'I don't know,' said the computer. 'The results of running a wormhole accelerator are unpredictable. That is why the experiments are taking place outside of the Earth's orbit.'

John had heard of the proposed wormhole accelerator experiments. They had something to do with finding out about the origins of the universe, but he had no idea what. In any case, it sounded as though they had best keep well away from them.

'You don't know much, do you?' John said.

The shortage of computer chips on Mars meant

that new computers tended to be built out of older machines. They were made of a patchwork of recycled materials, just like everything else. If an error or bug couldn't be fixed, the scientists found ways to work around the error instead. This had resulted in some very eccentric machines. They didn't always work in the way you expected, but they got there in the end. Usually.

'Claiming certainty where there is none is not useful,' said the computer enigmatically. 'We will reduce potential risks by travelling more slowly.'

The shuttle computer's lack of certainty wasn't very reassuring. John was about to ask more, but the computer abruptly announced, 'I will now fire the engines.'

'We're launching right now?' John suddenly felt nervous.

'I hope so,' said the computer. John didn't like the word 'hope'. The machine could have been programmed to at least sound confident.

'Don't you have to put us to sleep first?' he enquired, a hint of anxiety in his voice.

'No,' said the computer brightly. 'You need to be awake until we are in orbit in case something goes wrong.'

'Great,' said John, as he swallowed hard and lay back.

The engines roared, and the image of the skull, reflected above his head, started to vibrate. His hands gripped into fists as he felt the rocket starting to lift and the gravitational force pushing him down into his bed.

It felt as though a heavy weight was pressing down on his chest as they gathered speed. His fists uncurled of their own accord and his hands flattened to the bed. He felt his face pulled backwards. Even his eyeballs felt heavy, sinking back into his skull. The rocket juddered through the clouds, shaking him left and right.

Suddenly, the buffeting was gone. That must mean that they had cleared the atmosphere. Slowly the pressure eased off too. They were no longer accelerating.

'We are safely in orbit,' the computer announced. 'I am now attempting to prepare the correct mixture of drugs in order to induce a coma, from which I later hope to recover you without brain damage.'

'Terrific,' whispered John.

'This prevents me from having to feed and entertain you during the journey,' explained the computer.

John didn't like this situation one bit. 'Wake me as early as possible,' he said.

'Please stand by.'

John stared up at the jaws of the skull above him. Its teeth were magnified by the curved mirror. As the barbiturates flooded into his system, John felt the engines suddenly kick in again, jerking the craft away from Mars so quickly it felt as though he left a part of himself there. He lost consciousness wondering vaguely what real meat tasted like.

CHAPTER 13

JOHN MARCHANT: 2201

The stegosaur tasted rotten, but John knew he was lucky to have it. It could be his last meal for months. He sank his teeth deep into the pallid, long-dead flesh, forcing himself to swallow.

Incubating eggs meant staying close to the nest to protect them, and this had reduced the greatest hunter in the valley to becoming no more than a petty scavenger.

The closer to hatching the eggs came, the hungrier he had become. And now they were very close. His hunger made him weak and thin, and the desperation to relieve his starvation fought with the instinct to protect his eggs, each and every time he caught the smell of blood on the wind.

The scent of a fresh carcass was like a whisper on the air, calling all scavengers to feed. But the stench of this one was not a whisper. It was a scream that echoed through the trees. He'd followed it from the nest to the lakeside, and found the bloated body washed up on the shore.

Whatever had killed the stegosaur had done so some days ago somewhere upriver, and the lake's inhabitants had already taken what they wanted of the meat. The remains were waterlogged and rancid. Nevertheless, he hungrily tore off a chunk and lifted his head high to swallow it down. The maggots inside wriggled in his throat. *At least they're fresh meat*, he thought. If he could just stay alive for just a few more days, the eggs would hatch, and he could start to hunt again.

There was a loud squawk. He turned his huge head down to see a small dinosaur standing on the carcass in front of him, defiantly waving its thin claws. Its feathers were brightly coloured and bristling. He snapped at it, and it darted back just out of reach. It screeched again and swiped with its claw, grazing the end of his nose.

He took a step forward, and it jumped back. Suddenly, he felt a sharp scratch at his ankle. He swung his head around. Another of the little dinosaurs had nipped his leg, breaking the thick skin. He bellowed and launched himself after it.

Before he'd taken two steps it had disappeared into the jungle, and when he turned back, three more of its kind were standing on the carcass biting chunks out of it.

He ran at them, but they deftly leapt out of reach, circling around him, squawking raucously. Each time he made a grab for one, another would dart in behind him with a bite or scratch, only to skip nimbly back out of harm's way before he could bring his crushing jaws down on its back.

Each time he tried to return to feeding, the little dinosaurs would rush in to attack his legs. One even leapt up to grab a chunk of meat out of his jaws before he could gulp it down.

If he wasn't already weak and slow with hunger, he would have easily seen off the little scavengers. Right now, however, they were faster than him, and they had him outnumbered. If he didn't retreat the tiny bites and scratches in his legs would get worse. With the skin already torn, a lucky bite or slash could cut tendons or damage muscles, and a hunter with a wounded leg would not survive for long.

But if he didn't feed now, he'd be dead before the eggs hatched anyway. He tilted his head and eyed his attackers carefully as they stood in a row taunting him. Although he was nowhere near as strong as he once had been, his instincts were every bit as sharp. They stood between him and the kill, ankle deep in the water.

Suddenly, he gave a great roar and lunged at the scavenger on the left. It jumped out of the way, pushing its companions to the side. They scattered, slowed by the water around their feet. The one on the far right, furthest from the megalosaurus's snapping jaws, was struck hard in the side by the tail of its companion and fell, winded, into the water. Within seconds it was back on its feet and blindly pelting for the trees. John swung his massive head to the right and clamped his jaws shut with a spine-snapping crunch, hefting the dinosaur high into the air. At least this meat would be fresh.

Limping, carried his kill a little further down the lakeside to devour it in peace. It was small and bony, with precious little flesh to be picked from its bones, but it would do, for now.

By the time he'd finished, night was falling. He lowered his huge head down to the water to drink.

It was still, and his reflection was thin and dull. His eyes were sunk so deep into the sharp rings of their sockets he could hardly distinguish them. His face was a skull reflected back at him.

He moved his head, but the reflection of the skull didn't follow. It hung there, motionless in front of him. In the distance, there was a low, steady rumbling. It was very, very cold.

'I may have made a mistake,' said the computer.

John didn't move. His eyes slowly focused on the reflection above his head. His mind began to clear. Why was it so cold?

'You need to get up now,' the computer said without feeling.

John unfastened the drips from the bandages around his arms and swung his feet down on to the deck. It was so cold, the soles of his feet ached. His head was pounding and his lips were dry. *A glass of water and some slippers*, he thought, *would improve this experience no end.*

'Why is it so cold?' he muttered, his voice cracking.

'You asked me to revive you as early as possible,' said the computer. John hauled himself to his feet, and staggered to the cockpit window. Outside, thousands of stars stood out bright and sharp. He could see the sun's light reflected off the front of the ship, but the sun itself was out of sight to the left of his window.

'Where's Earth?' John scanned the scene in front of him. He'd never seen the planet as more than a dot in the sky. He looked for a blue and white sphere.

'I may have made a mistake,' the computer repeated.

'Why can't I see Earth?' pressed John, beginning to worry.

'Earth is here,' replied the computer. A blue neon arrow lit up in the centre of the window. It circled around a tiny star, only slightly larger than the other pinpricks of light surrounding it.

John felt his stomach tense. 'Why is it so small?' he asked cautiously.

'Because it is still roughly thirty million kilometres away.'

John stared at the tiny dot in horror. He felt as though all the air had been sucked from his lungs. He gasped, 'We're only half way?'

'You asked me to revive you as early as possible,' said the computer simply. It replayed him a recording of his own voice making the request just before he was sedated. 'Error checking reveals that I may have put too much emphasis on your wishes. This was probably too early.'

John staggered backwards and collapsed into the pilot's chair. His brain thought back to Mars, thirty million miles behind him, and then raced forward to the tiny dot of Earth thirty million miles ahead. The unimaginable distance filled his head.

'You mean we're still three months away?' he cried. 'Can you put me back to sleep?'

'No,' stated the computer.

He hesitated before asking, 'Is there enough air for me?'

'Yes.'

'Water?'

'There is enough water – '

'Good,' interrupted John.

'For roughly three weeks.'

'Ah,' said John, hope fading from his voice. So that was it. He would die of thirst in deep space. Back on Mars they had plenty of water. They had so much that they ran the base by splitting it into oxygen to breathe and hydrogen to give them power. John sat bolt upright. Could they do the same thing in reverse? 'Have we got hydrogen?'

'Yes,' said the computer. 'We have a lot of hydrogen.'

'Can you turn it into water?'

'Yes. Creating enough water is not a problem.'

John sighed in relief. 'OK, great. Do we have enough food?'

'No,' replied the computer. 'The drips you were connected to contain nutrients.'

'Enough to survive on?' asked John.

'Not in an animated state. They are only suitable for use in minimum energy-expenditure candidates.'

Back to square one. He would die, but more slowly. He tried a different tack. 'Can we get there any faster?'

'Yes, we can increase our speed. But this will result in passing close to the wormhole accelerator at a critical point in its experimental cycle. There are risks.'

'What does that mean?' asked John.

'Our universe is made up of a thin skin of order covering an ocean of chaos,' stated the computer. It paused, before adding, 'Probably.'

'And the accelerator experiments?' asked John.

'The accelerator experiments are designed to break through the skin,' it said.

'Just tell me what the risks are!' John was losing patience with the computer's vague answers.

'I cannot,' it said. 'If the result of an experiment is already known, it is not an experiment. Science is not a search for answers, it is a search for better questions.'

In the heart of the accelerator, power drawn from the sun charged great batteries, designed to focus impossible amounts of energy on the tiniest of things. Charged and drawn, particles hurtled forwards faster and faster in magnetically propelled arcs. Eventually, when they were moving so fast that their experience of time itself virtually froze, they were smashed into each other, shattering into sub-atomic shards. Particles that could only exist for a fraction of a second, particles that could be everywhere at once and particles that could defy time all flew from the impact and were captured and held, then collided again. They split into other particles, other combinations, divided, combined, fused and divided again into more and more exotic and impossible forms. And so it went on...

On the shuttle, John had no other choices.

'OK, just do it. Increase speed. Get me there as

fast as you can.' There was a brief pause, and the shuttle's engines roared into life. John could feel the ship starting to accelerate. 'Will this be enough?' he asked.

'It is very unlikely that you will complete the journey alive,' replied the machine. John fought the urge to smash his fist into the control desk.

'Well, at least make it warm!' he shouted. There was a whirring sound and warm air began to blow into the cockpit. 'Warm in a way that won't kill me,' he added guardedly. The computer kept quiet, but John thought he heard the whirring drop to a lower pitch.

He took a slow, deep breath and turned away from the tiny dot of the Earth, the blue neon arrow still pointing mockingly at it on the window display. He started to assess the cargo bay as his new home.

It was small. The floor was made up of a flat metal grating peppered with tiny holes. The ceiling was lined with lights and the walls were crowded and cramped with panels, wires and tanks. None of it looked edible.

The three beds, his own, and those of his parents were lined up at the end closest to the cockpit. He could see them both, still as death. Their faces were calm and pale. No sign now of the argument they'd had when he'd seen them last.

John walked past them down to the far end of the room. The skull sat staring out at him from the deep shadows. It had been strapped in to a secure crate that covered it on every side except for the front. He tapped on the case. It was made of a special new material that was designed to protect its contents from virtually anything it might encounter.

John patted the crate and wished as much care had been taken of him. But as he looked into the stone face, it seemed more fragile than ever.

'Well, I can't eat you,' he said out loud.

He noticed the three other crates stacked beside the skull. He knew what these were. Science stuff, mainly. He flipped the catch and opened one. Neat rows of Perspex boxes separated each object from the next. Most of the boxes contained rock samples. Each was packaged, carefully labelled and protected.

For John, they were like a catalogue of his life. Each different band of rock was a memory of his old life, and he remembered his parents' reaction to every one.

He picked up a box that held the first chip of gold found on the planet. Another contained a pebble of opal, worn smooth by an ocean that had dried up two billion years ago.

At the top of the crate was the latest addition to the catalogue – the rock he'd found on his last dig. He turned it over in his hands. The tiny burrow snaked through the stone, twisting and looping. Whatever had drawn the line billions of years ago, it couldn't be gravity or a rising bubble – it just couldn't.

Will it change anything? he wondered. Life on Mars, if that was what it was. Why should it? It was only the past, after all. He looked up at the huge skull in front of him. It didn't just look ancient. It looked old. Old, the way a person looks old. Somehow close to death.

'Did you change anything?' he asked aloud. 'If you'd stayed in the ground, would I still be here?' The skull stared blankly back.

His find would change one thing, he realised. John might not be the first Martian after all. He felt oddly sad. 'If this is a fossil,' he said to the skull, 'then your time's up. Nobody's going to be interested in you any more.'

He closed the lid and placed the small box back into its crate.

As he did so, he noticed one of the boxes underneath

it. This crate didn't just contain rocks. He pulled out the box. It was divided into a dozen compartments, and each held a sprinkling of tiny objects sorted into varying colours and sizes. Seeds.

Of course. The crops they grew at the base had been imported from Earth years ago. For decades they'd been cross-bred and refined for better yields under the base's unique conditions. Now scientists back on Earth wanted to study the results.

John couldn't believe his luck. If there was one thing that living on Mars taught you, it was how to farm. John was naturally good at it. He could grow just about anything, just about anywhere. He knew every species from its seed and every requirement to grow it. For every plant grown on Mars he knew exactly how much water it required, how much light, and what needed to be in the soil.

Quickly, he flipped open the box, and examined its contents. Carrots: they'd take sixty days to grow, no good. Lettuce: too big to grow enough to live on and not rich enough in vitamins. He riffled through the box, rejecting fruit trees, mushrooms and herbs.

Finally, he found what he was looking for. He took a handful of seeds and examined them closely. Bean sprouts would be ready to eat in a week. True, they wouldn't be much of a meal, but it would be something at least. Just enough to keep him going until the more substantial crops kicked in. He had time to grow small root vegetables. And there they were in the bottom of the tray like tiny fragments of bone – beetroot seeds. That would do. Beetroot and beans. Not much, but enough to keep him alive.

Life on the shuttle was lonely, hungry and slow.

His two companions, the computer and the skull, slowly fused in his mind. He spent long hours standing staring into the empty eye sockets and talking to the computer. When it spoke, its voice seemed to come from the skull's jaws.

The machine was eccentric, but over time he slowly began to respect it. Its job was to navigate the vast distances of space. In its world, the tiniest shift in the parameters of its calculations – a difference in weight in the cargo bay, the feather-light fluctuations in the solar wind – could multiply over time to throw out its projections of speed and direction. The computer couldn't be certain about anything because nothing was certain. Everything was subject to chaos and change, every law just a best guess.

John found himself obsessed with the skull. It had been around him for his entire life, watching him, but as the days wore on, he started to feel as though it had been following him for much longer. As if it had been with him for millennia. As though they were connected.

Every so often, he would open the crate to examine the rock he'd found on that last day, back on Mars, and trace his finger along the long, curved trail that ran across its surface. As he did so, he felt his link to the skull somehow fracturing. As if something was ending. Dying.

Around him, the vegetables sprouted, but they were not enough, and slowly John grew weaker and hungrier. Every day, he tended to the plants, his hands stained red by beetroot. Every night, he slept fitfully and dreamed of Jurassic forests and the blood-red tang of fresh meat.

And slowly, day by day, week by week, month by month, the tiny dot of the Earth grew larger and bluer in the cockpit window.

CHAPTER 14

JOHN MARCHANT 2201

'It's time,' said the computer. John woke instantly and sat upright. The hunger in his stomach was intense, and it was all he could do to climb to his feet. He struggled into the cockpit. The Earth seemed huge in the window. He could make out the continents, clouds, and the soft blue glow of the atmosphere.

'We have slowed for our approach to Earth,' said the computer.

Today, it would be over one way or another. If all went well, they would land and he would walk out of the hatch to start his new life. First, however, they had to pass the accelerator and its mysterious experiment.

'Where is the accelerator?' asked John. A neon arrow highlighted an area of the window. John could just make out a dark grey ring against the black sky. It looked quiet enough. 'Is it finished?' he asked.

'No,' said the computer. 'The final collision phase is due to begin imminently.'

'What does that mean? Should we wait?'

'The final phase of the experiment will be triggered automatically when enough particles have been collected,' it said. 'It could be a few seconds or several weeks.'

'We'll go now', said John. He knew he wouldn't last a couple more weeks, let alone several. This was not the time for the computer's philosophical dithering. Besides, he had been practising manoeuvring the shuttle for months. He grabbed the controls and pushed them forward. The engines growled as they started to accelerate towards the planet.

Inside the experiment, something triggered. Ranks of tiny cells, each holding its own subatomic prisoner in magnetic isolation, clicked open. Released from captivity, each particle, an exotic refugee from an unimaginable realm, claimed its freedom. They flooded into the chamber at the heart of the ring, spinning, spiralling and arcing with alien energies.

The shuttle was within a few hundred miles of the accelerator when it blew. A sudden flash of blue light blinded John, and as his vision cleared, he saw the enormous ring start to fall in on itself. Around it, light bubbled and fizzed. A fury of chaos seethed and folded. Tendrils reached out from the centre and flicked into space. John fought to keep the shuttle steady as it shook and rattled as though flying through a storm.

A spark of blue foaming fire swept out in front of them and the shuttle tumbled over and over, spinning out of control. John pulled back, hauling the controls against the spin with all his strength.

Slowly, the ship steadied.

He looked back. The explosion was fading. Its fury was gone, and the void of space was once again darkening to a sooty black.

'Is it over?' he asked the computer.

'No.'

John looked again. At the centre of where the ring had been, bubbles were forming. They seemed even darker than space itself. As he watched, they floated outwards. Most burst in seconds, but a few of them drifted out into space towards them.

'Wormholes appear to have been successfully synthesised,' the computer continued. 'They are extremely unstable and must be avoided.'

John steered the ship sharply away, yet the bubbles seemed to follow, as though the shuttle had a kind of gravity, pulling them in. He weaved left and right trying desperately to shake them off, and one by one, the bubbles burst.

Finally, just one wormhole remained. It was following his every movement. John looked into the monitor showing the rear of the shuttle.

The dark bubble filled the screen.

'What will happen if it catches us?' he yelled.

'We will either be crushed to a single point,' said the computer calmly, 'or transported to the other end of the wormhole.'

Neither option sounded good to John. 'What can we do?' he cried, flinging the shuttle to the left and then to the right to try to shake the bubble off.

'I don't know.' The bubble was still closing in.

'Can we close it?'

The computer thought for a moment. 'A large mass dropped into it might close it.'

John leapt up from the cockpit. 'Take control,' he yelled.

He looked around the cargo bay. In one corner, a mechanised space suit stood, its magnetic feet clamped firmly to the floor. John fumbled desperately with the catches as the ship weaved from side to side, up and down. Finally, he was in. The helmet hissed as it filled with air and the suit clanged into life.

'Open the airlock doors,' John shouted above the sound of the engines.

'Opening the inner and outer doors simultaneously will cause complete depressurisation of the vessel,' replied the computer. 'Do you wish to continue?'

'There's no time,' cried John. 'Just do it. Now!'

The inner and outer airlock doors started to swing slowly open. Instantly, the cargo bay was in chaos. The plants that had kept him just alive were torn out from their roots as the air was sucked out of the shuttle. Everything loose was being dragged towards the doors. Only the transport crates and his parents' beds remained bolted in place. Everything else was flying out into the void.

Slowly, one step at a time, he clanked the suit across the metal floor. Outside was an emptiness so huge, it made John's head swim. The bubble was so close he felt he could almost touch it. He forced himself to look away.

There was only one thing on board large enough to stand a chance of closing the wormhole. He raised the suit's metal arms and grasped the edges of the crate containing the skull. He pushed as hard as he could. The bolts securing the crate to the floor finally gave way and the skull began to slide towards the open door.

Outside, the wormhole was almost touching the ship. Its surface reflected the light from the engines. The ship bucked and strained, as if against an immense gravitational field.

As he pushed, John stared into the skull's huge dark eyes. *I'm sorry*, he thought, as he shoved it across the metal floor. *I have no choice.*

Finally, summoning the last of his energy, he sent it tumbling into the oily blackness with one immense, final push. The instant the skull disappeared into the bubble, the wormhole collapsed into itself and there was silence.

'Shut the doors,' cried John, as he stared into the empty blackness. He felt a strange sense of loss. Somehow, it was as though neither the skull nor the wormhole had ever existed. At the same time, he felt as if he were somehow the creature's killer.

As the computer guided the shuttle through the Earth's atmosphere, John looked out of the window on to a slowly unfolding blue map. Oceans spread out in front of him, green and yellow landscapes dotted with the pale grey sprawl of mankind's habitation.

His parents were being revived and soon he would step out of the hatch and enter this brand new world. And then he would eat meat.

He looked back to the empty space at the back of the cargo hold.

'Where did it end up – the skull?' he asked the computer.

'I don't know,' the machine replied. 'Wormholes don't just traverse space, they travel across time too. A better question would be: "when did it arrive?"'

'When did it arrive, then?'

'I don't know,' said the computer.

EPILOGUE

High above Earth, a swirling black bubble grew suddenly out of the darkness of space. A battered crate span out of it and was instantly caught in the planet's gravitational field.

As the wormhole closed, the box tipped over and over, down towards the green and verdant world below.

The stone skull's jaws gaped wide and its empty eyes glowed red with the heat of re-entry. As the crate burned and fused around its contents, protecting it as it was designed to do, it slowly began to disintegrate, searing into a shower of bright, tiny rocks that trailed behind the skull like a fiery tail.

Glowing and terrible, the monster screamed towards the Earth, a burning, roaring predator from the sky.

Somewhere below, beside a lake in a warm Jurassic forest, a female megalosaurus broke off from her hunt and turned her eyes up to face her killer.